THE MEADOW

THE MEADOW

Ann Thompson

Copyright © 2007 by Ann Thompson.

Library of Congress Control Number: 2007902840
ISBN: Hardcover   978-1-4257-5503-4
            Softcover   978-1-4257-5502-7

All rights reserved. No part of this book may be reproduced or transmitted in any form or by any means, electronic or mechanical, including photocopying, recording, or by any information storage and retrieval system, without permission in writing from the copyright owner.

This is a work of fiction. Names, characters, places and incidents either are the product of the author's imagination or are used fictitiously, and any resemblance to any actual persons, living or dead, events, or locales is entirely coincidental.

This book was printed in the United States of America.

To order additional copies of this book, contact:
Xlibris Corporation
1-888-795-4274
www.Xlibris.com
Orders@Xlibris.com

38736

CONTENTS

1. Amy's Meadow 9
2. Dan's Meadow 19
3. The Decision 26
4. First Encounter 31
5. A Watchful Eye. 36
6. Communication 41
7. Dan Confides in David 47
8. The Picture 52
9. The Book 56
10. Amy Confides in Nikki 61
11. The Investigation 65
12. The Portrait 69
13. The Revelation 72
14. Town Talk 79
15. Dan Departs 83
16. Young John. 88
17. The Painting 94

BEYOND THE MEADOW

Chapter 1 101

DEDICATION

To my wonderful daughters, Margaret and Lynne, who found the idea of me writing a book quite exciting and who remained supportive throughout the entire process. Their help in changing my raw ideas into a delightful story and their constant reassurance that writing this book was the thing to do really helped me. Thank you, girls.

To my husband, for all of his encouragement and the patience with which he endured my hibernation in the computer room. He was my sounding board, my editor, and my support. Thank you, my love.

To the delightful stranger I met on a plane who had much more confidence in my book than I did at the time. Just knowing she was out there waiting to see the finished product kept me going for many nights. Thanks, Sonja.

WAITING

BY John Burroughs

Serene, I fold my hands and wait
Nor care for what nor tide nor sea
I rave no more 'gainst time or fate,
For, lo! my own shall come to me.

I stay my haste, I make delays;
For what awaits this eager place?
I stand amid the eternal ways,
And what is mine shall know my face.

Asleep, awake, by night or day,
The friends I seek are seeking me;
No wind can drive my back astray,
Nor change the tide of destiny.

What matters if I stand alone?
I wait with joy the coming years;
My heart shall reap where it has sown,
And garner up the fruit of tears.

The waters know their own and draw
The brook that springs in yonder heights;
So flows the good with equal law
Unto the soul of pure delight.

The stars come nightly to the sky;
The tidal wave unto the sea;
Nor time, nor space, nor deep, nor high,
Can keep my own away from me.

CHAPTER 1

Amy's Meadow

"New York City! That's where we should go! We could stay a few nights, take in the theater, and sample the cuisine. Oh, Joe! It would be such fun."

"You know I can't go to New York, Amy."

"That's always your answer. Just take three days off. We haven't gone anywhere together since the children left home. If I called this afternoon and made the reservations, we could leave on Wednesday; and you would be back to work by Monday. They wouldn't even have known you were gone."

"I won't leave the project in this stage. The team would not be able to finish without me." Joe's response was emphatic. Amy knew Joe wasn't going to change his mind, but she counterattacked anyway.

"That's always been your excuse," Amy snapped. "It's always been that you are the only one in the lab who would know what to do. I find that hard to fathom. It sounds to me more like an ego trip or an excuse not to be with me."

Joe softened. "I'm truly sorry, Amy. Honest, I am. I feel a terrible sense of responsibility for this project. It was my brainstorm; and if anything went wrong, it would put us back to the beginning. I just can't take the chance. When this project is over, then I promise, we will get away for a while."

Amy gave up. It was always like this. Joe had always been this way about his research, and nearing retirement age didn't change that for him. He was so deeply involved, and he loved what he's doing; so she couldn't imagine him ever retiring.

She and Joe appeared to have a rock-solid marriage—the all-American Dream. They had met during their senior year in college. Joe was a very serious biochemistry major, who was determined to be the first to find new breakthroughs in cures for all incurable diseases. Amy was a budding new artist. Their worlds and ideals were completely different. Still, Amy admired and loved Joe, and he felt the same about her. They would both laugh about being polar opposites and assure all their friends that opposites really did attract.

"I'm going to be a famous artist someday, and Joe is going to find cures for almost everything," Amy would confide to her roommate.

"How many children do you want?"

"I don't think we will have time for children. We will be too busy being famous and will be busy traveling around the world together."

Just after graduation, they married and felt as though they would conquer the world together. They each had grand plans for both their individual lives and their lives together. Amy was an inexperienced artist, but she had created some pieces that were very strong. She had an ability to convey through the canvass thoughts and emotions to the viewer about what they saw. Joe, who had always wanted to do research, took a job with a pharmaceutical company in Ohio where he was granted a wonderful opportunity to pursue his dream. Neither Amy nor Joe felt the need to set boundaries on the other in their pursuit of a career. Amy was painting and successfully selling much of her work at a local art gallery. Joe was deep in a research project. Life was exactly as they had dreamed it would be.

Two years into her art career, Amy discovered she was pregnant; so she traded art for cooking and cleaning and being the full-time mother and the taxi driver. Three boys and one girl—Nikki, Jeremy, Josh, and Joe Jr.—overran her life with football, math club, dancing, soccer, and piano lessons. The list was endless. Her hours were completely devoted to children and their activities. It wasn't the life she had planned, but she loved her children very much, and she took motherhood seriously. Her boys were fun, and she enjoyed them; but her daughter was her best friend.

Joe's love of research took him away from his family. Amy was proud of what Joe was accomplishing, and she was happy that he had such an opportunity to pursue his life's dream. He had made a name for himself in the field of medical research, and his list of publications was long; but Amy missed having a partner. She complained when Joe did not attend a single football or soccer game. He missed dance recitals, piano concerts, and school plays. She felt he should play a more important role in their life. She and Joe still loved and admired one another, but they had drifted far apart; and she longed to have that closeness back once more.

Amy occasionally complained about his absence and lack of participation in family affairs, but many of her friends played the same role—that of a "married" single mom. Eventually, she accepted their relationship. They were, after all, an average family living the American Dream.

Sometime during midlife, Amy began to ache—not just the normal end-of-the-day ache, but one that kept her awake at night and never went away. Her energy level went down, and with it her lust for life. Amy went from one specialist to another and endured one test after another. After months of testing, the doctors had eliminated everything but fibromyalgia. It was a disorder that made her body uncomfortable and depleted her energy, but at least it wasn't deadly—just painful. She vowed she would learn to live with it. That proved to be easier said than done. Mornings found her barely able to get out of bed, and she was moving very slowly. By midafternoon, her energy was depleted; and she would stop to rest.

The children who had kept her life and art career on hold were now grown and had finally moved away from home. An empty nest at last. The boys had all married and settled within a hundred mile radius of home. Nikki had not been so lucky. Every job she sought seemed to take her farther and farther from home. Amy missed her best friend. "Can't you find some type of work here in Ohio?" she had asked Nikki over the phone. "I miss my best friend."

"I miss you too, Mom, but there don't seem to be any jobs for me available in the area. Maybe someday there will be."

"I don't really have much hope of that happening."

"Me either. I prefer to be somewhere warm. I'll find a nice warm place to live, and you can move with me."

Amy laughed. "Sounds wonderful, but I would have to leave your father in a lab here in Ohio. I can't imagine ever prying him lose from here."

Amy gave up hope of any kind of life or travel with Joe. He was too deeply rooted in his work now to get away even for a few days. She understood how Joe felt about his research, but her knowledge of how he felt didn't fill the emptiness she felt without him. When they married, they both had talked of big career plans. Hers had simply been delayed; that was all.

She tried to return to her art, but the pain that was in her muscles and the weariness that she constantly battled almost brought her creativity to a halt. It was that soreness, which had gotten Amy involved with meditation. She had tried every thing: exercise, painkillers, diets, carrot juice, and acupuncture. If anyone had suggested it, she had tried it; but nothing had given her even a hint of relief from the constant and increased throbbing in her muscles or the weariness that plagued her constantly. Several different medications had seemed to help at first, but gradually, all the symptoms would return. Joe had gotten involved as well. He had brought home several different mixtures from the lab—of what, nobody knew—but Amy took them all faithfully. Nothing was working.

Susie Daniels was not only a good neighbor but also someone who had been her confidant and friend for many years. She was very involved with health food and meditation. She had always claimed those were the two keys to getting through life, and it seemed to work well for her. She was a tall slender woman who never seemed to get ruffled or excited. She had been a wonderful calming force in Amy's life especially when she was annoyed with Joe for working such long hours. Susie always interceded on his behalf and managed to calm Amy's ruffled feathers.

She always sensed when Amy was upset. "What now?" she would ask over tea or lunch.

"It's Joe again. He has started another new project and doesn't come home until well after midnight."

"He always does that with a new project; you know that. He will get home earlier after the project gets off the ground."

Amy groaned. "I know, but the kids had so much homework last night we couldn't get it done. I needed him to be at home. He never seems to be around when I need him."

"Now, Amy," she cajoled, "you have a good guy. He always comes home, provides amply for you and the kids, and loves you very much."

Amy knew Susie was right. She was glad for her friend. Somehow she always added reason to Amy's world.

She had involved Amy in yoga classes. She hoped the yoga would have a calming effect on her old annoyances and help with the new pain problem she had developed. It didn't really seem to help much, but Amy enjoyed the classes and continued going. She and Susie would meet for coffee every Wednesday and then attend the nine o'clock yoga class. She was even starting to learn a few meditation techniques. Susie had read about a new combination of vegetarian diet and meditation that was supposed to help fibromyalgia patients.

"Why don't you try it?" What can you lose?"

"I've tried everything else. I guess it can't do me any harm."

"I have a couple of great books on Zen and different types of meditation. I will bring them over tomorrow, and you can get started right away."

"Thanks. If it works, I will owe you."

"I'll bring along a couple vegetarian cook books as well. You will need them."

So, as with each new suggestion, Amy read Susie's books and bought several more books on meditation that she thought looked interesting. She gave up meat and started in earnest on the last program that she had any hope in for relief.

Amy didn't realize there were so many different mind exercises one could do. There were chanting exercises, humming exercises, and out-of-body exercises; the list was endless. She read all the pain relief exercises and at last settled on one that seemed especially delightful.

It was an exercise from Susie's books that prompted the creation of the beautiful spot. The book had given detailed directions about how to create a place of your own. Amy had worked for several weeks in quiet thoughtfulness on just the right vision that would suit her needs. Finally, she had it. It was her place—her special spot. She had awakened in the middle of the night with a vision of exactly the type of place she had been searching for. It was like she had dreamed about it, but it didn't really seem like a dream. Wherever it came from, it was perfect. It was a beautiful meadow with grass that was soft and dry—never prickly or damp—and always green. The sun was always shinning, and there was always a soft breeze blowing—one that rustled her skirt as she walked along. A beautiful babbling brook flowed along past the meadow to a small falls, which dropped off into somewhere below that Amy never saw. A friendly big shade tree stood ready to provide a shady area to sit and rest. Even the tree did not feel rough when she leaned against it—just firm and comfortable to her back. Best of all, of course, there were no insects. The beautiful meadow could not have been more perfect. Of course, it couldn't; she had created it in her mind. It was her source of refuge to escape from all her cares and pains.

In the exercise, she was supposed to find a way to rid herself of all the aches and pains, all the emotional stresses, and any sadness she might be feeling. Amy chose the small twigs or leaves that continually floated by. They would be excellent to carry off her woes. One twig, one care; one leaf, one pain. She always wore the same thing in the meadow. It was a white dress, soft and flowing, with a scoop neck for comfort. It seemed to be something between a nightgown and a dress made for perfect comfort and definitely suitable attire for such a lovely place. She always had a large-brimmed white hat. She was never sure how that got in her picture, but she did remember having one that looked like it years ago when hats were the rage; and it was her favorite. Maybe that was how it got there. Usually, she was carrying it along with her for it was never on her head but always with her. Always she was barefoot. Of course, that is how she had been most of her life, and since she had created the meadow, there was no worry about stepping on anything. The grass felt wonderful to the bottom of her feet—soft and relaxing. Always it was the same routine. She would approach the tree, and soft breeze would be flowing through her hair and across her face—warm and gentle. It was as though the breeze knew exactly what she needed, and it was trying to blow away her pain. She would walk slowly up to the tree, then sit and lean against it like an old friend. Then one by one, she would place her cares and pains on the leaves and twigs and watch as they floated off, feeling every part of her mind and body relaxing. The object of the exercise was that once they were out of sight, she would let go of each of them in her mind. The amazing result was that the pain would float over the falls and Amy would actually feel pain free long enough fall asleep. One of the suspected causes of her disorder was a lack of sleep. This exercise seemed to be giving her a more restful sleep.

After a few weeks, Amy had mastered the ability to visualize the meadow and place each care on the leaves quite easily. She found that it was not only possible to relieve the pain long enough to find sleep, but it seemed to be helping some during the day as well. At least, if the pain wasn't gone, the meadow was so relaxing that it simply put her to sleep and made her wake feeling pleasant the next day. Either way, the exercise was helping.

Nothing she had done before had ever done much good, but the meadow seemed to be the key. It was such a beautiful spot; in fact, she had painted a striking picture of it and had hung it on their bedroom wall. Joe appreciated the picture as well. He was sure it was one of Amy's best works. It was her favorite too. Just looking into it often relaxed her even without the meditation. What a beautiful place, she would often think,

What a shame it isn't real.

The meditation and the meadow had helped relax Amy enough that she now could start painting with some seriousness. The aching and exhaustion were far from gone, but it was improving and her mind and eyes were beginning once again to see art and beauty in the world around her.

She had always loved old barns, so they were an easy choice for the subject of her art. She would travel through the back roads of the state and take snapshots of every barn she could find, and then she would put them on canvass or paper. There were dozens of old barns in the countryside around Ohio. Some almost fallen down; some still standing majestically as a testament to the days gone by. The older the barn, the more character it had; and the better Amy liked it. Many of the old barns had burned down, fallen down, or been carefully taken down to reappear as paneling in beautiful homes. Whatever their fate, over the years many had disappeared and were now gone forever. She enjoyed seeing them preserved there on canvass so that they would forever stand in her paintings.

Life was going nicely. Her pain seemed to be under control, her pictures were selling, and the children were on their own. The only drawback was that Joe was remained deeply involved in his research projects; and now that they were alone and had some time they could have spent together, he was still married to his work. Amy felt like she was on the back burner. It had been that way for most of their married life. Joe had his work; Amy had the house and children and what little was left of Joe after work. The family had kept Amy busy, and she managed to fill her loneliness with their activities and love; but now, she was by herself all day and late into the night. She was beginning to feel a deep discontentment.

Then one day, the phone rang.

It was Joe's secretary, making a frantic call to Amy. Joe had collapsed at work.

"Where is he now?"

"They called an ambulance and are taking him to the Methodist Central emergency room."

"What happened?" By now, Amy was starting to sound frantic.

"We don't know. He had been fine one minute, leaning over his microscope. The next minute, he stood up to go for an aspirin and simply collapsed."

"He is on his way to the hospital now. I can see the ambulance pulling out," she had said. "Could you meet them at the emergency room?"

Amy called her sons en route to the hospital. Two of them managed to reach the hospital almost as soon as she did, but Joe was dead before they could load him in the ambulance. Amy never got to say good-bye. Sitting there in the hospital waiting room, she tried to remember if she had even said good-bye when he left this morning, or was it like many of the other mornings when they never really even noticed each other?

Josh and Jeremy were there when the doctor came out.

"I'm so sorry. We did not have a chance to save him. The test showed a blood clot in his brain."

"How could that be? He was only sixty years old."

"It can happen. A weak spot somehow that just gives way. There is not usually any warning with those things."

"He never even had a bad cold that I can remember. I don't think he was ever sick a day in his whole life."

"Unfortunately, these aren't the result of illness. They are usually a defect that has been there a long time and just never detected."

She and the boys sat on a bench in the hospital still stunned and not really able to get up and leave.

"He can't be dead. He was in the middle of a wonderful research project."

"We will take care of everything, Mom. Let us get you home for now and get hold of Joie and Nikki."

Amy sat at the table in the kitchen alone. He just couldn't be gone, but he was. Now for the first time in her entire life, Amy was alone—suddenly and totally alone. This was different. Joe wouldn't be coming late at night, waking her up when he climbed noisily into bed. It wasn't the same as just being in one part of the house at night and him in another. She was now in the house all by herself. She had gone from her parents' home to the dorm to married life with children. There had always been someone in Amy's life. She had complained about him working such long hours and being gone so much of the time, but he had always come home at night. There were always signs he was there—dishes in the sink or half a cup of coffee on his desk. Now it was deathly quiet in the house. Nothing moved except Amy. There wasn't even a goldfish swimming around in a bowl. Amy had avoided taking in any pets because she had not wanted to have to care for anything else. Now she wished there was another living, breathing creature in the house besides herself. This was going to take some serious getting used to. Even the meadow was not enough to fill the void Joe had left.

Amy's sons came by as often as they could and tried to call her as well, but it was Nikki she turned to. Her daughter was a stunning-looking tall slender young woman with her mother's black hair and dark eyes. She was now approaching forty; and although she had brought home many a man for her mother to meet, she had not chosen to marry any of them. She had remained close to her mom by telephone even though distances had kept them apart.

She had floundered on the sea of life's indecisions for years, trying first one thing then the other. Nothing seemed to give her the satisfaction she was seeking. While the boys had all married and settled close to home, Amy's only daughter had been the one who wandered afar. From the East Coast to the West, and still nothing seemed to work. Her last move had been to Charlotte, North Carolina. There she had opened a small shop. She was quite happy in Charlotte and was well pleased with the success of her business.

The small scrapbook shop she had opened five years ago had become quite a popular place. Nikki had expanded the walls twice now and was offering more and more merchandise. It was a charming little shop with scrapbook materials, small decorative collectibles, candles, and other assorted merchandise.

"Move to Charlotte, Mom. The weather is wonderful here, and there are lots of old barns you haven't painted."

"I never lived anywhere but here. What would I do there?"

"You could help by working a few days a week in the shop."

"I might enjoy that."

"You could continue to paint. I will hang them in the shop"

"I don't want to ever live with one of my children."

"That's OK, Mom, we can find you a nice home that is smaller but suits your needs. Please come. I need you here, and now with Dad gone, there is no reason you can't move."

In the end, the solitude was more than Amy could bear. As soon as she could, after setting their affairs in order, she sold their house and moved to North Carolina to be close to her only daughter and her best friend.

She painted landscapes and barns mostly, but a few flowers and birds would also appear on her canvasses. She displayed some of her art in Nikki's shop, and found she was able to sell as many pictures as she had time to create. She also had a few paintings hanging in the gallery next door to the shop. She had always loved to paint, and now it kept her fingers and mind busy. It was fun to be able to enjoy her daughter again as well after many years of living apart.

Like Nikki, Amy found Charlotte the perfect place to live and work, and the area around the city gave her a new selection of old barns. She had bought a small home that was new and easy to care for, and working in the shop gave her some human contact. She was painting and keeping herself busy. The emptiness caused by the loss of Joe didn't go away, but she had finally accepted that he was gone. Her life was now on track.

Amy's biggest problem now was that her muscle disorder had grown worse. The pain and the loneliness sent her to the meditation spot more and more often. The peace of this place and the relief from the pain was such a blessing that she began to make it a practice to take out time every afternoon now for meditation. It had always been her habit to use the meadow for relieving the pain at bedtime, but it was quite pleasant to stretch out in the middle of the afternoon and drift off into that lovely meadow where she never felt pain or loneliness. There in the meadow she was at peace with her soul.

CHAPTER 2

Dan's Meadow

Dan was a tall muscular boy with a handsome face that rarely showed a smile. He had light brown hair and soft blue eyes that revealed a kind and tender heart. His strong, solid jaw line and the deep cleft in his chin added to his rugged appearance. Most of the local girls had their eyes on him and were always available for him, but Dan found most of them to be silly and immature. His mother had always said he had been born an old man with a frown on his face and it only deepened with age, but Dan was hardworking, honest, and kind.

Growing up in a small community had some perks, but it also has some drawbacks. Dan had lived near this small town north of Charlotte since as long as he could remember. His family was well known, and they knew almost everyone there. He had gone to school with most of these people, gone to church with them or done business with them. They were friendly and always willing to help each other. It was similar to living in a big family.

The biggest drawback was the gossip. It seemed to go on from morning till night. The church socials buzzed, the general store buzzed, and the ladies clubs buzzed. Most of it was just friendly buzzing, but Dan had never appreciated it.

"Now, Dan," his mother would say, "the ladies are just having fun. They don't mean any harm to anyone. None of us have ever said mean things."

"I know, Mom, but you know how much I hate thinking that I might someday be part of that conversation."

His mother laughed at that. The thought of her oldest son being part of the town gossip amused her. "Your brother might someday be the topic of conversation, but I can't imagine them ever discussing you. It is just our harmless way of keeping up with each other."

"I know it is, but I never like hearing it."

Quiet and serious beyond his years, he had found an older woman from another county more appealing to his somber nature. He had met Sue May at a church function during his junior year in high school. She was a teacher in the next county and had come to visit her Aunt for a few weeks. They became fast friends, then sweethearts. Her involvement with Dan caused her to extend her visit for the rest of the summer.

Six years his senior, Sue May loved Dan very much. She knew people talked about her and the great age difference, but Dan's maturity made him appear much older than he was. She had never been a beautiful woman, but her gentleness and kindness had drawn his attention. She had chosen to become a teacher because of her love of children. A dozen, she thought, would be how many she would like for her own. Dan felt the same about children; and shortly after he graduated from high school, they married and moved onto a part of the family farm located just north of Charlotte.

Dan farmed the land, and Sue May continued teaching. When he wasn't farming, he was making beautiful hand carved pieces of furniture, and selling them in town. They both worked hard making their life good, but the one thing they both wanted most, they never got. The dozen children never came.

By the time Sue May turned forty, they had given up their dream of having children and contented themselves to life as it was. But on her forty second birthday, she realized that she was pregnant. Neither of them voiced their fears, but a first-time pregnancy at forty-two was risky. Dan was worried; Sue May's excitement over the pregnancy overcame her fears.

"This may be our only little one, Dan. I hope he is just like his father."

"I just hope this whole thing goes well. You know I am worried about you."

"It will be fine," she would assure him. "You just need to have more faith. It is the child we have always wanted."

The pregnancy was hard. She spent most of the last four months in bed. The frown on Dan's face grew even deeper as the weeks went by. The delivery did not go well and in the end, both baby and mother were lost. Dan was distraught. He had lived with Sue May since he was eighteen. What would he do now without her? He was still young when Sue May died, but the dreadful loss and the fear of experiencing it again had caused Dan to avoid another relationship; so he had lived the last twenty years alone.

He had his beautiful farm nestled in the hills of North Carolina—quiet and peaceful. It was part of a larger farm that he had grown up on. He was the eldest of four children, but he had only one brother still living. He had lost one sister to influenza and another to childbirth. David was ten years his junior, but he had always loved him. They had always been best friends. He still had David close by, and he still had the farm and his beautiful hand carved furniture to keep him busy. He never really felt lonesome out here in the woods. It was good land to farm, and plenty of wood to make furniture with. He was never one to be idle or let himself feel the loss of his family, so he spent his days in quiet solitude.

Dan had wonderful neighbors. They were always stopping by to check on him and chat awhile. Hardly a day went by that someone hadn't stopped in to have coffee, chat, and see what he was working on next. His brother lived only a few miles down the road as well, and he stopped every chance he had. Dan was grateful for their concern and their company, but he was always glad when their visits were over. He had never been one for small talk. Solitude suited him better.

There was an especially beautiful area on his farm—a meadow. It had a beautiful brook flowing along side it with a small waterfall that dropped into a larger lake below his property. He could see the meadow from the house, but it was otherwise isolated from the road. It was such a peaceful place that he had arranged to have his wife and baby boy buried there. The sounds of the brook and the falls were so serene, and he often sat under the old willow oak tree and visited with them.

Dan had always felt some strange attachment for the meadow and had just kept it mowed and untouched by crops or farm animals. It was restful and quiet there—a place that could relax even the most trouble soul and because it was always visible from the house. Dan would often gaze off through the trees into the meadow when he rested on the porch.

Dan had started his day earlier than usual. He wanted to get the barn cleaned out and rearranged. His furniture making had overrun the shed, and he needed more room in which to work. The barn was old, but it still kept out the elements. It would make a comfortable place for expansion. By midafternoon, he was ready for a long break, so he made himself some coffee and settled in the big swing on the front porch.

Gazing off into the meadow, he was just beginning to relax when he thought he saw someone out there. Surely, he was wrong. No one could get to the meadow without walking past the house. It might have been possible to reach the meadow by wading across the brook, but no one was living on the farm behind him. He walked out to the fence. Yes, there was definitely someone out there. It was a woman walking through his meadow. She wore a dress, a flowing white thing that looked more like a nightgown or some type of choir robe than a dress. He watched spellbound while she walked slowly along as though she knew her way well. She sat down under the big tree, gazing contentedly at the brook and not moving or making a sound. He was sure she was unaware that anyone was watching her. Who was she? Where had she come from? He wondered why he felt such an unusual stirring at the sight of her; something deep within him awakened. He was sure he had never seen that lady anywhere before, and yet he felt an immediate attachment. He looked both ways down the lane to his home to see how she had come. There was no apparent method of transportation. When he looked back, the lady was gone; she simply vanished.

Every day for the next week, he checked the meadow, wondering if he would see her there again, but no lady appeared. Just as he was about to give up and convince himself that he must have seen a ghost, she reappeared. It was long past Dan's bedtime, which was close to midnight. He had been unable to sleep, still wondering if the creature he had seen was real or if he had simply imagined her. Maybe she truly was some form of spirit. Maybe it was after all his wife. He always dismissed this theory because the lady he had seen in the meadow looked nothing like his dead wife. At least, a ghost should resemble the dead, and she neither looked like Sue May nor carried herself in the same way. She just could not possibly be her. If she was not Sue May, then she had to be someone else, and therein lay the mystery.

He had come out to sit on the porch for a while. The evening was warm and still. He was hoping that the quiet of the evening would clear his mind and let him finally sleep. The meadow was awash in moonlight. The sight of it, quiet and still, had a calming effect on him. He had almost forgotten about the mysterious lady when suddenly his heart gave a jump. He felt the flush in his face that goes with a sudden rush of excitement. There she was! She was walking along in the same white dress, and the light from the full moon made the white dress appear even more eerie than Dan liked to admit. Almost like a replay of the first time he had noticed her, she appeared in almost the exact same spot. She walked to the old willow oak tree, sat softly down, leaned against the friendly old tree, and seemed to be watching the brook go by. Maybe she was his dead wife after all. Sue May had loved that meadow and had often gone to sit under that same tree to watch the brook go by.

No, he didn't really believe in ghosts, and this one looked much too human. If he was seeing Sue May, he couldn't imagine why she would wait twenty years to come back to the meadow. Surely, she would have been there all along, and he had never seen this vision before. He had often sat in the meadow himself or watched it from the porch. He was sure this woman could not have come to the meadow without him seeing her. Maybe this was just his imagination playing tricks on him. Dan had always been a serious person, not prone to fantasy or make-believe games, but now, an overactive imagination made more sense than anything else he could formulate. If not, then who was she, and how did she just appear and disappear from his meadow?

If she wasn't a fantasy, there was the dilemma of what he should do next. He considered going down there, approaching the lady and demanding to know just what was going on. He could insist on an explanation as to why she was trespassing on his land, and what was she doing out alone especially this time of night. It was past midnight, and no self-respecting lady would be out unescorted at that time of night, especially wandering through a field.

Half a dozen plans of approach went through his mind as he sat there; but with all these thoughts of what he should or shouldn't do, he couldn't move. He just sat there, watching her almost afraid to breathe for fear she would disappear again. Just the sight of her sitting there in the meadow made his heart happy. It was the first time in a long time Dan had felt that happy. Truth was, he didn't know if he had ever felt really happy. Content would be more the description that suited him, he thought, but now he actually felt happy. He realized she was not a young thing. From that distance he guessed late '50s, early '60s, but her hair was still dark in the moonlight, and while she was not thin she wasn't too heavy either. She was tall and carried herself nicely, giving the appearance that she knew his meadow and was very comfortable there. He couldn't see her face or eyes, but her body language told him she was totally at ease there in the meadow.

The longer he watched, the stranger it seemed. It was interesting, he thought, but she didn't even seem to notice that it was the middle of the night, nor did she seem to be aware that he was sitting on his porch not far from her watching. She just sat there leaning against the tree; she seemed to be studying the brook as it flowed by. Maybe it was the moonlight that gave her sight, but Dan had a strange idea that for her it was not nighttime at all. He enjoyed just sitting there on the porch, watching her appear so completely at home in his meadow. It made him feel peaceful as well. He felt so comfortable with her being there in his meadow, and he sensed there was some strange bond between them. He forgot all about his plan of approaching her; and the next thing he knew, the sun was coming up. The lady in white, of course, was gone.

Some days would go by, and she wouldn't appear in the meadow at all. Then she would be there every day for a few days in a row. She would often sit there for quite some time, but then she would just be gone. How did she leave without him seeing her go, and where did she go?

It was very odd he thought, that he had never noticed the lady before, for she seemed to appear more and more often. He found himself checking every day at different times to see if she had arrived. He wondered what he might do when she came next. He had a deep desire to look into her eyes, for he was sure that the peace he felt from watching her was there in her eyes. He felt an increasing need to see her face to face that grew stronger every day, but the fear of scaring her off kept him on the porch and at a distance.

Perhaps it was a fear of disillusionment. What if he approached her, and then he realized she was only his imagination. The sight of her so stimulated all of his senses that he would miss the vision if it was no longer there. Possibly, there was a fear of rejection as well. If she was just a lady from somewhere around the area, maybe she was married; and speaking to her would drive her away. If he introduced himself to her and she was single, perhaps she would not be interested in him at all and would move on to someone else's meadow for her walks. So for now, he was content to watch her from afar. He wasn't willing to take a chance on causing her to disappear just yet. He was starting to grow accustomed to seeing her there. He even began to feel like he had company on his farm for the first time in years. That wasn't such a bad thing to have some company either.

He made some mental notes as to what time she would appear, hoping maybe there was some pattern to this. There did appear to be a pattern. That made it easier to be there when she came. Usually, it was midafternoon and late at night. Midafternoons were easy for Dan, but he had always been an "early to bed, early to rise" type of person. Being awake at that time of night was a little harder, but he would manage it somehow. Once he thought to himself about how afraid he had been as a child when someone told ghost stories. Now he chuckled to think how brave he had grown.

The more often the lady in white appeared, the more Dan longed to have some type of communication with her. He was sixty—not growing any younger and way too old to go out courting, he thought. Now, seeing her there in his meadow made him realize what he had missed all these years living there by himself. He had never felt a need or a desire to remarry, but now this wonderful creature stirred a longing in him to have some companionship and love in his life again. How could he reach her? He had convinced himself that if he just walked up to her she would disappear from him forever. What could he possibly do? How could he approach her? He wasn't sure now how long it had been since he first noticed her being there, and he wondered how long she had been coming there before he had noticed she was there. Worst of all, he had no way of knowing how much longer she would continue to come to his meadow. He didn't even know if she was real or just something he had created in his mind perhaps out of the need to fill his loneliness. All he knew was that somehow he had to reach out to her. He had to understand the source of her peace and where she came from. He was totally convinced that it would not be possible to feel such a strong emotional pull toward an imaginary creature. Somehow he was positive that this woman was as real as he was.

CHAPTER 3

The Decision

Dan's brother stopped by on a regular basis just to check on his big brother and be sure all was doing OK. Since Sue May had died, David worried about Dan living out on the farm alone. David lived on the west side of the farm only a few miles from his brother's home, so he made it a weekly habit to stop by for a visit. This week Dan had been anxious for him to come because he wanted to share these strange sightings he was having. He felt the need to discuss them with someone he could trust. What would the town think of him if they heard he was out here watching a make-believe woman come and go from his meadow? Now that would set the town on its heels for sure, thought Dan with a smile. He could still hear his mother, "Your brother might someday be the topic of conversation, but I can't imagine them ever discussing about you."

"Well, Mom, you should be here for this one," he said to himself out loud.

He had several friends who came by on a regular basis, but none he trusted like his brother David. Dan had gotten the looks in the family, but David had gotten the personality. He had always been the one who had all the fun. He laughed easily, and he was never bored. He always found life to be a pleasure no matter how it seemed to be going. He enjoyed a good story and tried anything new and had a zest for life that was contagious. That zest had gotten him into a few scrapes when he was younger, but Dan had often envied his lightheartedness and wished he could be more like that.

David had fallen in love with Becky when he was in the second grade. They had dated through high school. They had married as soon as graduation was over and reared three children. He and Becky were best friends and soul mates. Dan was sure they were the only couple on earth who seemed as in love on the day the last child left home as they had when the first child was born. Now with the kids all grown and gone, they were enjoying each other very much.

Dan had always been serious, down to earth, and hardworking; and he didn't have much time for fun. Now he felt very foolish being the one who was having visions of fair maidens and falling in love with ghosts. Maybe a young man would be dreaming dreams but not a man of his years and maturity. He would never have believed that something like this could have happened to him; and certainly, it would be a hard sell to his brother.

David found Dan waiting on the porch for him with coffee in hand. Usually he had to hunt him down somewhere on the farm. Waiting with the coffee, though, wasn't what peeked David's interest. It was the broad smile that was on Dan's face. He couldn't remember the last time he had seem his big brother smile. This was a different Dan than he had seen last week. Truthfully, he had been noticing a change in his brother for the last couple weeks. It had just been so gradual that David had dismissed it, but today it was so obvious he couldn't help but comment on it. His older brother, who had probably been born with a frown and retained it for sixty years, was now smiling. His face had somehow been altered from a serious worried face to a pleasant, almost happy face. How could that be? It had to be a woman behind the transformation.

"Say," he said, "you are looking like you came to life out here. Has that Melinda Bartell been coming by? She was asking about you the other day down at the store."

Dan smiled. "I wish it were that simple, David. I could tell you about it, but you wouldn't believe or understand it. I'm afraid that I don't know if I believe or understand it myself just now. I was hoping that you would make it by today though because I would like to get your opinion on something."

David stopped and studied his brother. He knew instantly that Dan wasn't kidding, and he was interested in any good story especially one he might not believe. He always loved a good challenge especially when it was intellectual.

"OK. give! What's up out here that's got you seeming so different? I'd love to hear about this one." He took the coffee his brother offered and settled himself in the swing on the front porch.

"I'm waiting all ears and with an open mind." He wasn't prepared for what he heard next.

Dan spoke slowly as though he were measuring his own words and trying to say them in a way they would make sense even to him.

"Do you believe you can create something in your mind that is so genuine you can't tell if it is real or fantasy?"

"I suppose one could do that. I always had a wonderful time in life that I never felt the need to create any fantasy. I bet there are a lot of people who do, though. I don't know about the not-knowing part."

"Not really a fantasy with imaginary creatures or faraway places but a person; I mean, someone who can give you such an incredible peace in your heart that all your loneliness just disappears even just a mere sight of him or her."

David wasn't sure how to answer that one. If anyone could create that, it would have been him, but his brother Dan? Now that was a stretch. It would have been quite the accomplishment even for him; still, he didn't want to close this conversation by saying no. He realized that would just cause Dan to silence his thoughts, and it was obvious that something had happened to him; and he was wanting to discuss it. He wasn't sure he wanted to say yes to that question either. That might encourage some fantasy that his brother obviously already was having.

"Well, I sometimes see Bradley coming down our lane—happy, healthy, and alive. It makes my heart sing until I realize that Bradley is gone from us forever. So I supposed that you could do something like that. Maybe it is Sue May that you believe you are seeing."

Dan was almost sorry he had asked David that question. His brother's eldest son had been thrown from a horse some years ago and had died. He and Becky were still grieving the loss.

"No, she isn't anyone I have ever seen before, but she is female. She comes to the meadow, and sits leaning against that tree, watching the brook. I know that Sue May used to do that same thing, but I am sure this is not her ghost. I have never gotten close enough to see her face, but I can tell from here that she is totally at peace there—resting and happy. It makes me feel tranquil just seeing her there. I feel some type of strong bond to her for some reason, but I'm afraid to approach her. I just stay put here on the porch and watch her. The next thing I know, I blink; and she is gone. I am not sure if she is existent or just my imagination. If she is real, I'm wondering where she comes from; and how she gets out of the meadow so quickly. If she is my imagination, I am wondering why do I feel such a strong connection to her, and why don't I just leave her there all the time for my viewing pleasure."

"Maybe she is coming across the brook from the other farm."

"I thought of that, but I don't believe it would be possible for her to get across and back so quickly that I wouldn't see her coming or going. So what do you think?"

David didn't have any answers for those questions. This certainly wasn't the story he was expecting to hear from his big brother as to why he was smiling lately. The one thing he did know was that his brother wasn't crazy. Dan was the soundest person he knew; solid, serious, and hardworking. He couldn't imagine his brother making up something like this, or anything else. His serious nature didn't lean itself to imaginary stories. He also knew his brother wasn't kidding with him. He honestly believed he saw this woman—whatever or whoever she was—and there was no doubt she was making an impact on him. It was obvious that something about his big brother was very different.

"How long has she been coming to the meadow?"

"I don't know," Dan admitted. "I have been watching her now for a while. I'm not even sure how long."

"Have you tried to make contact with her?"

"No," Dan said sadly, "I have been afraid to for fear of scaring her away. What if I approached her and she rejected me? I couldn't bear that."

"Well, I suppose that the best way to find out what she is all about is to simply walk down there and ask her. If she is something you have imagined, then surely you will realize it when you touch her and talk to her."

"Yes, that has to be the answer. I think direct contact would be the next step. I must decide how I should do that."

"Has anyone else ever seen her?"

"No, and it is interesting that you ask. Ivan and Jake were both here last week when she appeared, sitting right here on the porch with me. I asked them if they saw anything in the meadow, and Ivan gave me one of those looks that suggested I might be seeing things or needed new glasses. I decided not to mention I could see a woman."

"That was probably a smart thing. Jake would have been at the next checker game telling all the boys about it, I'm afraid."

"Well, at least if that happened and she was from around here, it would flush her out."

David was feeling more than a little uncomfortable with all this talk about ghost or imaginary ladies or whatever it was that his brother was seeing in the meadow. His sincere hope was that when Dan went to touch his ghost it would disappear, and he would realize that it was just imaginary and come to his senses. He realized his brother had expected more help and advice from him than he was capable of giving just now. He needed some time to give this some thought and figure out what might be going on.

"I will try to ask around the county and see if anyone new has moved on to the farm behind you. Maybe she is just visiting someone in town."

"That could be. I never thought of that."

"Let me know how it turns out. By the way, did you need anything from the store? I'm headed that way."

"No thanks. I have to deliver two chairs over there tomorrow. I can pick up anything I need then. I think you are right too. I need to pinch myself and find out if I'm dreaming here or if there really is someone in the meadow."

"I don't have any answer for you, Dan, but I am convinced that you should confront her and find out who she is."

"Yes, direct contact; that has to be the answer. Thanks, David, and please keep this under your hat. I wouldn't want the whole town thinking I have lost it out here in the woods. Guess it's OK for my little brother though. See you in a week. Hopefully, I'll have this mystery solved by then. Have a safe trip." Dan turned to go back inside.

David watched after his brother as he went back in his home. He had an uneasy feeling about leaving him there alone with all that was going on. He was hoping this vision would just disappear, and his brother would come to his senses. He had a lot to consider before he came back. The whole concept had hit him unexpectedly. By this time next week, he was sure he would have all the answers.

CHAPTER 4

First Encounter

Dan realized David was right. A direct approach was probably the best way. He had to find out if the lady in the flowing white dress was just some vision he had created or if she actually was as real as she felt to him.

He tried to devise a plan of approach. The meadow was quiet; there were hardly any leaves to rustle or twigs to snap, just soft green grass. He would wait until she crossed the meadow and leaned against the tree. By now, Dan knew every movement she would make; for it was always the same. Once she was seated, he would just walk up to her from behind and take his chances. At least that way, she would not escape until he was close; and he would be able to see where she went when she left. His heart raced at the very thought of it. He hadn't been so excited over a female encounter since he was fourteen. How could this make him so giddy? He felt like a teenager again. It was a new sensation for Dan since even as a young man, he had never seemed to get too excited over much. Still, he decided, it was a nice feeling.

The whole watching and admiring and meeting of this woman in his meadow had apparently taken over his mind and heart. It was something he had to try even if she never returned. He had to look into her eyes just once, speak to her, and touch her. Maybe she wasn't actually there; maybe she's only a figment of his imagination. It was time he found out for sure. He also knew he had raised concerns in David by telling him about the woman before he knew anything about her.

Maybe being out there on the farm alone all these years had caused him to create this wonderful illusion there in his field. He had never considered himself lonely on the farm. The solitude suited him. Still, if he had now created someone to keep him company, why would he send her away? No, he was sure in his heart that if he had just created her, he would leave her there all day every day because by now he was growing accustomed to seeing her there so content and so at home, resting in that spot. He realized he had started missing her when she was gone. Definitely, if she were his creation, he would never move her from the meadow. She had to be real.

He had never been one to imagine anything. Play for him had been building things or growing things. He had left the imaginary play to David. Now he just needed to stroll through the meadow and ask this woman who she was and where she was from.

Now that he had made up his mind to approach her, what if she didn't come again? What if she never came back to the meadow after she saw him? What if all those sightings had just been his vivid imagination? What if he approached her, and she disappeared because she had just been a vision? The list of what-ifs was endless, but what choice did he have now? He had come too far now to back out. He had waited too long for this chance not to follow through. It meant too much to him to see her face to face. He didn't want to just continue watching from afar. He had become deeply entangled with this meadow and this lady. Now, he had to move on with his emotion. His heart raced. His mind swirled with hope and fear—what was next? With his mind set, ready to make the move, his biggest fear was that she might not appear. He sat nervously on the porch with coffee in hand and his heart in his throat, waiting and hoping, even urging her to be there this afternoon.

There she was. She had come right on schedule. He was very relieved to see her. After all that great planning he had done, if she had not shown up today, by tomorrow he might have not been able to go through with the meeting. He changed his approach plans at the last minute and chose not to come into the meadow from behind her. Rather, he decided he would just walk across the meadow from the same direction where she seemed to always come from.

He hoped with all his heart that she would not see him coming and would decide to just leave. Somehow he no longer felt the need to try to sneak up on her. Suddenly, he no longer had the dread that she would disappear. Deep in his heart, he knew that she was going to be glad to see him. For some unknown reason, he was sure they were meant to be together, whether she was real or imaginary, and she would not move away from him. Weeks of uncertainty gave way to self-assuredness.

So he waited and waited while she came slowly across the meadow and sat down under her tree. Once she was seated and watching the brook, he made his move. Slowly, he crossed the meadow. He could see her eyes fixed on his every move. Normally, he would have been both nervous and embarrassed by her stare, but his eyes locked with hers; and he felt a deep connection. Whoever she was, Dan already felt very comfortable with her.

She was watching him but made no move to get up or leave. Now he was close enough to see her face. It was a nice face—soft and friendly; she also had black eyes with sparkle and love in them yet a haunting of loneliness. She had short black hair with some gray that curled softly around her face. She looked exactly as he had pictured her from his porch, and the peace and tenderness he had expected to see in those eyes was definitely radiating directly toward him. She smiled at him with some wonder in her eyes as though she couldn't believe anyone else would have entered her private spot; nevertheless, she didn't move a muscle. She simply sat and watched as he came closer and closer.

Amy had never had another person in her meadow or in her meditation. *Odd*, she thought. Why would she conjure up a male person in her special spot? This was her spot for getting away from everyone, not getting close with someone. Still, the sight of him coming toward her didn't alarm her in the least. After all, this was her meadow—her fantasy, an invention of her mind, and a place to rest her painful body and lonesome heart—nothing more; her physical body wasn't even really here. So she simply watched him approach her with slight curiosity, wondering what her meditative state was about to have him do.

He was a nice-looking man, probably about sixty years old, Amy thought, with graying hair and nice facial features that were softening with age. He was tall and muscular for a sixty year old. He looked like an outdoor type who worked in construction or something similar. His clothes were different from any she was used to seeing—rugged, outdoors type of clothing; nothing new like jeans and T-shirts, but they fit him well and showed a body of a man who had done physical work in his lifetime.

There had never been anything about this sort of occurrence in any of the study books Amy had bought. Several had given the example of creating a special place to relax in, but none had even suggested that someday another person would show up in that place.

Still, Amy liked the total look. She thought it was interesting that she would imagine a man who looked like this for no one she knew fit his description. He had just appeared there in her mind. Strangely enough, she felt drawn to him as though they had known each other for a long time. It was an interesting feeling, she thought, since he had to be imaginary, yet he looked and seemed so very real.

Should he speak to her? Should he simply sit against the tree with her and say nothing? Dan couldn't even bring himself to even say hello. He just sat down beside her—almost but not quite touching. He had a chance to study her more closely. He had never seen her before in that area—of that he was sure. He had never seen a dress or hat that looked anything like hers either, and her feet were bare—no leggings and no stockings. Her hands were soft like a woman's who had never done hard work.

Where on earth did she come from, and how did she get here? She had no shoes and no apparent mode of transportation. She had to have gotten here somehow. Her bare feet were soft and clean. No, she didn't walk here from very far away. Who on earth was this? Surely, she wasn't just a figment of his imagination, for here he was sitting right next to her; and she seemed very much alive.

No, by now, Dan was positive that she wasn't a vision or some invented creature. This lady was real, and the feelings of magnetism were certainly real as well. He was so drawn to her that he felt as though he was becoming one with her in some unexplainable way.

There were so many questions going around in his head that he couldn't ask any of them. He just sat, breathing in the peacefulness around the two of them and feeling a strange contentment just being next to her. He was so very grateful to David for pushing him into this meeting. He had been so afraid to come close to her, and yet here they were close enough to touch; and she was no vision. She was a wonderful, peaceful, creature who Dan felt he could be close to forever.

Suddenly, he jerked. He must have dozed off. Before he even opened his eyes, he already knew. She was gone. How long had he been there sleeping? When did she leave? Why hadn't he talked to her, found out her name, where she came from, when she might come back? More importantly, why hadn't she spoken to him?

With a heavy heart, he walked back up to the house. He had never thought of it as being lonely, but now suddenly, the whole area seemed bleak with loneliness since the lady in white was gone. Even his lovely meadow seems bleak and forlorn with her gone. When would she ever come back? How had she made such an impact on his life in such a short time? He made a quiet vow to keep a daily vigil and to speak to her if she ever came again. How could he have been so foolish as to just sit there when he had the chance of a life time and let it slip through his fingers?

Dan's consistently logical life had suddenly turned into just a mass of questions and illogical thoughts. This type of experience might have happened to anyone but not to Dan. How foolish was this to feel such deep attachment for someone he had only met once and to whom he had never even said hello. Dan remembered how hard it was for him to talk to Sue May when they first met. He had never been good at small talk, but Sue May had put him at ease quickly. Interestingly enough, this woman had watched him come up to her, sat with him, but never said a word.

He was hoping his brother had either found someone in town who had a visitor, or had come up with some ideas about what was happening to him.

The night was long, and sleep just wouldn't come.

CHAPTER 5

A Watchful Eye

Amy awoke the next day with a strange but peaceful feeling.

Wasn't that just the strangest thing, she thought to herself. *I have been going to that spot in my mind for some twelve years now and never before did I ever put a man there or anyone else for that matter. I wonder what on earth came over me. He was so very real, like I didn't put him there at all; but he came from somewhere else. Where on earth else could he have come from?*

The meadow was just Amy's imaginary spot. No one else could get into her mind without her putting them there. While it was a bit unsettling to have had someone intrude on her private spot, even in her mind, it was a little exciting. Of course, the big question still remained: why didn't she have him talk to her? It would have been even nicer if he had maybe put an arm around her and held her. She would have loved to have cuddled up in his arms and felt someone else's strength around her for a change. She was sure she must have conjured him up because it was the first time she had seen him, and suddenly, she felt a surge of emotion that made her realize she felt somehow very attached to this man—real or unreal.

A funny little tremor of excitement ran down her spine, one she had not felt since back in high school days. "Oh, for goodness' sake," she said to herself, "you are much too old to be feeling this way. Get your canvass out and get busy with your painting. You have orders that are two weeks overdue now, and you have plenty to do on it."

Still, the interesting man in her meadow haunted her throughout the day. Several times during the day, she found herself gazing off into space with paint brush in hand. He did not look like some modern-day man. He appeared to have come from some other time. What he looked like or where he came from wasn't her primary focus. Not even the question of how he got into her meadow bothered her. The important thing was how she felt about him—this man who had just appeared. How could she feel drawn to a vision she had created—to someone she had only seen once and had said nothing? And yet, she was.

The idea of feeling attracted to any man aside from Joe was completely foreign to Amy. Their life had not been wild and romantic; and she had often been annoyed by his absence from the home, but Amy had loved Joe. She had never considered being anything but faithful. Now, for the first time since her senior year in college, Amy felt attracted to someone other than Joe. She didn't feel the usual attraction felt for a good-looking man in a restaurant or a shopping mall. This was almost some form of unnatural attraction—a daunting feeling they had known each other before and been more than friends.

By two o'clock that afternoon, her curiosity had just gotten to be more than she could endure. Her hope was that meditation would take her back to the meadow; and she would somehow manage to envision the same character from the day before. What fun! A little excitement was a good thing for an aging lonely old lady. Her mind began to sift through the possibilities of her imagination. What if she got there as usual and couldn't make him appear? What then? Well, the meadow had been all she needed before him. It would be again after all. Why did she think she needed a man now after all these years? Her life was on track and going well. OK, maybe she was just a tiny bit forlorn and feeling her age.

Well, either way, she was going to stretch out and do some meditating. If he reappeared, that would be wonderful; if not, she back needed a rest anyway. The canvass she had started this morning was taking shape faster than she had expected, and she could spare some napping time.

Amy lay down, making her as comfortable as possible; she believed she would return and find the same man waiting for her. Unfortunately, she never got to the meadow. Sleep overtook her first. She awoke disappointed for the missed opportunity, but at least, she was rested; and her pain had eased.

Several days went by with the same results Amy was just pushing her self so hard that by the time she put her head on the pillow and thought of the meadow, she was asleep. Perhaps by the end of the week, she could slow down. She would have to be less tired, if she was going to get back there. She was very anxious to see if the man would be in the meadow again, whoever or whatever he was. She somehow felt they were meant to meet. It was a feeling they should have known each other before and had now been united in the meadow.

Several days went by, and the woman did not appear. That had happened before, but now Dan was worried. He was afraid maybe his visit to the meadow had caused her to go away. He worried now that she might not ever come back. His greatest fear was the possibility of losing the one thing in his life now that truly brought him happiness. The fondness that he felt for this woman was undeniable but unexplainable.

When the lady did not reappear for several days, Dan poured himself into the work he had to do. He had some chairs to finish for a customer and lots of work around the farm to do. It was enough to keep his body busy, but his mind wandered to the meadow constantly. He tried to work as close to the house as much as he could so as to keep an eye open in case she returned.

Next to his brother, Jake was the best friend Dan had ever had. Friends since childhood, he came by the farm several times a week to check on things and be sure all was OK. Jake was a big talker and knew everything that happened in his county and the surrounding ones. Dan had no intention of confiding in Jake about the woman who was coming and going so unusually, but he did have something he needed from Jake.

This afternoon, Dan saw him coming and was glad for the company. He didn't want to let on that anything was different, but he knew Jake got around all over the county; and if anyone new had moved into the area, he would know.

After they had gotten their coffee and settled on the porch for a chat, Dan brought up the subject. "Have you seen or heard of any newcomers in the area, Jake?"

"Like what kind of newcomers?" Jake looked a little suspicious. Jake was always that way. He prided himself on knowing every secret in four counties. Maybe it was the way Dan had said it, or maybe it was the smile Jake had noticed creep across Dan's face a few times lately that made him wonder why he asked that question.

"Oh, I just thought I saw someone walking through the meadow the other afternoon. I wondered, maybe someone new had moved into the old Jackson place on the other side of the creek. Don't often see anyone strolling through my fields."

"Nope, to my knowledge, no one new has moved in anywhere around here lately. Maybe it could have been someone from down closer to Charlotte, looking for some new property to buy. Lots of new folks are moving in there these days. What'd they look like?"

"It was a woman. I wasn't close enough to really see what she looked like, and she was gone before I knew it. She didn't appear lost, so I thought she might have been someone living around here I just hadn't met yet."

Jake arched one eyebrow. "Maybe you are just seeing ghosts."

Dan tried to sound amused. "Maybe, but not many of those are roaming around the local farms in the middle of the afternoon."

"Nope. Guess night is their time for strolls."

"It doesn't really matter. I don't mind having people on my property, you know that. I just thought someone new had moved into the area that I didn't know." By now, Dan was working hard at sounding nonchalant, and he wasn't sure he was succeeding.

"Well, I'll keep my eyes open for any newcomers and let you know. Meanwhile, if she comes back, just go down and ask her who she is and what she wants. You might find out before I do."

Jake had already heard that David was asking around, looking for some new woman in the area. Something was up out here on the farm, but he realized Dan had said all he was going to say. He would just keep his eyes and ears open.

Dan was hoping he had not aroused any suspicions. He never liked keeping secrets much, but this one was something he was sure he shouldn't be discussing with anyone. He was wishing his brother would come that afternoon. He had so much to tell him.

"I will keep you posted, Dan," Jake hollered as he went off down the lane.

"Thanks, Jake."

David didn't come by until the end of the week. Dan was anxious to report the latest updates to him.

"Hey, brother, how is your lady friend?" he asked as he came up the steps and took a seat on the porch.

Dan didn't smile. He didn't even answer.

"Awww, I was just kidding with you. I've been asking around, and no one new has moved into the area that I have heard about. Has she stopped coming? Was she just a dream?"

Dan stopped working on the chair he was finishing. "No," he said, "I did what you suggested. I went down there the last time she came. I walked right up to her. She never said a word, and you know, I found that I couldn't say anything either; so I just sat down there beside her and soaked up the peace and contentment that seemed to flow from her. I don't know if it was her or the meadow or a combination of both, but whatever it is, I sure enjoy the feeling I got just being out there with her."

"Did you touch her?" David asked.

"No, I guess I was afraid to, but I can tell you now that if she ever comes back I am certainly going to. Now I know for sure she is real. It was so restful, sitting there with someone else I went right off to sleep; and when I woke up, she was gone."

David didn't know exactly what to say next. Certainly, his brother would be the last to lose his senses—his big brother Dan, the one always with a slight frown, who was always on the serious side of life and never had time for fun or imagination. There had to be someone or something that was real for him to be so intense. David would sure like to see this lady himself.

He still didn't have any answers for his big brother about who she might be or where she had come from. David caught Dan up on all the latest local gossip and how his life was going then got ready to leave. He wanted to get his load delivered and get home before dark.

"Well," he said "if you ever see her again, let me know. I'd like to see her myself. Next time, big brother, at least say hello to the woman." He picked up the chairs that David had finished, loaded them in the wagon, and headed into town to deliver them to the general store.

Dan finished up his last chair by three that afternoon and sat down on the porch with some tea for a rest. He took a few moments to review the last few weeks of his life, and then, he smiled.

"Yep," he was talking to himself out loud, "this whole experience must be good for me because here I sit, smiling away at nothing and waiting for someone to just appear here for me."

Amy finished up her duties at the shop by two and headed home for her bed and the meadow. She wasn't so tired this afternoon, but her body was exceptionally uncomfortable; and she needed the relief that the meadow gave her. Of course, there was another reason for going to the meadow. She was determined to get back there and see if the man would appear again. This time she would talk to him. That might explain what he was doing in her meadow. She had to try not to be too excited or have too many conflicting thoughts; meditation was harder when that happened.

CHAPTER 6

Communication

Meditation is a clearing of one's mind of all thoughts except the desired ones. Normally, that had become easy for Amy; but now it wasn't as easy. Now there was someone else involved in her secret place. She had taken some medicine to help ease the back pain, and it was starting to take effect. That always helped considerably because often times it was hard to make your mind clear with the severe pain. Now it was even harder. She decided that if she was ever going to get to the meadow, this time she was just going to have to imagine it with him there or at least with him coming to the meadow shortly after she arrived. Otherwise, she wasn't going to be able to picture the meadow at all.

So she pictured the meadow as usual and pictured herself walking to the tree as usual, then she sat under the tree as usual; but before she could envision him coming toward her, there he was, doing exactly that. His collar was open, and his shirt sleeves were rolled up like he had been working on something. This time, he was hurrying toward her. His anxiousness made her frown slightly. No one should hurry in her private relaxing spot. He must have sensed her dismay, for he slowed to a walk as he made the final ten yards or so.

Dan had been sitting there, resting on the porch and keeping a close eye on the meadow. It was just about the time when the lady had appeared before, and he was not going to miss any chance he had now to speak to her. He glanced at the list in his hand of the orders for chairs he had yet to fill. When he looked up, there she was, moving quietly and slowly across the meadow to the tree. He was on his feet, off the porch and halfway across the meadow in just about a single bound. Suddenly, he noticed the frown on her face. Maybe he was scaring her, moving in such haste, so he slowed to a walk as he came in closer. This was his big chance, and he wasn't going to miss out.

Immediately, he spoke, "Hello, I'm Dan Kerr."

His voice was deep and soft with such a Southern accent that he would have put any stranger at ease. Amy would have expected nothing less. He had said such a simple sentence in such a hurry as though he might not have the chance to say anything else if he didn't hurry and get that out.

Dan, now that was interesting. She didn't know a single person by the name of Dan. Where could she have gotten that one? This was a relaxation exercise. Talking during it was defeating the purpose of relaxing, but somehow that seemed OK because she wanted to know something about this man and how he got in her meditation spot. Like he might know why she had put him there; besides, she didn't remember ever feeling this relaxed since she had started this practice some twelve years earlier.

"Hello, Dan," she said, "I'm Amy, Amy Brandson. Where did you come from?"

What a silly question. She felt very foolish the minute the sentence left her mouth. She knew where he came from. He came from her mind. Somehow she didn't want that for an answer. It was almost inconceivable that she would have suddenly, after all these years, put this man in her meadow. It was like her mind was rebelling against having him there, and yet part of her mind was thrilled to find him there. It didn't really matter because there he was standing in front of her and actually speaking to her.

Dan slowly lowered himself to a sitting position beside Amy. Now he was directly in front of her and could look into her deep black eyes. No, this was no imaginary being. He was quite sure of that. She was as real as he was.

"I came from the house up there." He pointed to his home up the hill.

Funny, she had come here so many times and never seen anything but the meadow, the brook, the falls, and the trees. That was all she had ever envisioned. That was all there was. Or at least that's what she thought. Where was the house really? She couldn't see one no matter how hard she looked. All she could see were the limits of the meadow her mind had set many years ago.

More to the point, she asked again, "Where did you come from, and how did you get here?"

Amy found the whole conversation very strange so far. Could this man really live close to the meadow somehow, and was he really a flesh-and-blood man? He didn't act like someone she had made up, and now he didn't look like it either. More important than how he looked like was the feeling she was having when she was close to him. It was as though they had known each other for a very long time and somehow were meant to be together.

"Is there really a house over there?" Amy wasn't in a hurry to explain to this man how she actually came to be in his meadow.

"Yes, just on the other side of that fence. It is my home."

Amy peered to her left, but she saw no fence and no home. All she saw were trees along the edge of the meadow.

"So did you just walk down here from the house?"

"Of course, now the question is, how did you get here?"

He wasn't going to give up, so she tried to explain to him how she actually did get there. "This is where I come to find peace and freedom from pain. She told the details of what the meditation exercise was all about. I made up a beautiful, peaceful place for my mind to escape to;and this was it. When my body is beyond uncomfortable and my mind is on overload, I escape to here and find peace. This meadow is my very private, imaginary spot.

Sitting so close to her and looking deep into her eyes, he realized that she must think she was telling the truth. There was no hint of dishonesty behind those deep eyes. Dan was still looking at her as though he had heard something he couldn't believe but did accept as true anyway.

"But you didn't make this up, Amy. This is my meadow. It is not an imaginary thing. It belongs to me. It has been my property for some thirty years, and it belonged to my father before me."

"Where are we, Dan? Where is your farm located?"

"Just north of Charlotte."

"Charlotte, North Carolina?"

"Yes, is there another Charlotte?"

Amy was taken aback. So the physical meadow could not be far from where she lived, or could it? Somehow it seemed very far from her.

She reached out and gently touched his arm. He felt warm, strong and solid. She felt as though she was losing her focus. How much longer she could stay in a meditative state to keep herself in the meadow? She knew that once the exercise relaxed her sufficiently, she would drift off to sleep and leave the meadow far behind.

Her mind was reeling. She was sure sleep would not come now, but she was surprised that the shock of finding a real man and a real meadow in her contemplative state didn't stop her concentration. How could all this be possible? She had invented this spot. There wasn't any such spot this beautiful in the real world. Still, she had never had anything like this occur before in all her years of meditating. How could she have imagined something that was so exact as a real place, and where was this place anyway? It was so rustic, and civilization seemed so far away. Amy's ordinary world had suddenly been turned into an extraordinary world.

Dan was still frowning at her in disbelief. He had heard her explanation but wasn't sure he could believe it. "So you simply will yourself in and out of my meadow?"

As bizarre as that sounded when someone spoke it out loud, that was almost exactly what Amy did. She willed herself into the meadow; but usually, sleep took her out. How could she make this man understand? How could she make anyone understand the way she came and went from this place? Right now, she couldn't even make herself believe something like this could happen. Her imaginary meadow had become physically realistic, and she was there.

If it really was an actual place, how did she get here? When she had first started meditation exercises, she thought that the out-of-body thing would be just the greatest experience. While she had tried and tried for out-of-body experiences, it had only happened once, and it was nothing like this. She remembered her body had seemed to float above the bed, but that sensation had only lasted for a minute or so; and then it was gone. Now she was somewhere completely away from her home and bedroom and in the company of someone else. She was sure stranger things had happened to others but never to her.

Dan was sitting beside her quietly, turning all the information Amy had given him over and over in his mind. He did not doubt what she was saying, and yet, how could anyone make up his exact meadow? Was anything like that even conceivable? Well, he concluded in his mind, it must be possible; for one minute she was here, walking in his field; and the next moment, she was gone. He had begun to realize this was something more than a ghost or just a simple person wandering into his meadow. He wasn't sure why this was happening, but his mind and heart told him that their meeting had a specific purpose; and this must have been the only way. He was still very unclear as to how she could get there.

"How does that work?" he asked again. "How is it that you just appear here, and why do you just disappear?"

Amy could tell Dan still wasn't convinced. She wasn't sure she was convinced either, so she tried again to give him a more detailed account of what happened in her meditation exercise.

"I lie down to ease the pain in my back, and then I envision this beautiful place, which I was sure I had made up in my mind. I put each pain and care on a different leaf that floats by; and when they go over that falls, I am at peace. I stay until my physical body actually goes to sleep, I guess. That part I am a little uncertain of. I always assumed that when I went to sleep, I left the meadow since I could never remember any of this being in one of my dreams. That, simply stated, is how it happens. I never thought it was complicated before; and certainly, I don't know how you happened.

He was quiet for a while, then he asked, "Why are you dressed like that?"

Amy laughed softly more to herself than out loud. She had never really thought much about her wardrobe. She had not selected what she wore that she could remember. When she visualized herself there in the meadow walking, she was wearing that dress and carrying the hat. She had often wondered herself why that attire had been selected.

"I'm not sure. I always seem to be wearing this dress and carrying this hat. I had one of these wide-brimmed hats in my younger days when hats were popular. I always loved this big ol' hat. Maybe that is why I have it. I'm honestly not sure. Somehow I never wear it; just carry it along, but I never seem to be here without it."

She watched him sitting there, thinking about what she had just told him. He had a strong physical appeal for his mature years. She was worried about how much longer she could will herself to stay before her body at home fell fast asleep.

"I don't always come every afternoon," she said hurriedly for she wanted to communicate her time frame to him before she was jerked out of the meadow and back to her own room. "I do come every night at bed time. I guess I don't stay long then, but I am always here for at least a short time. My bedtime, I'm afraid, is usually close to midnight."

She was holding her breath, hoping he would want to come back and meet her in the evening but afraid to ask that of him. She didn't even know if he could really come back to the meadow or if he, like herself, was pulled in and out of it.

"I have been watching you for several weeks now. I realized there was some schedule to your coming and going. I never knew the reason for it."

"I never saw you before the other day."

"I have stayed on my porch, watching. I didn't want to scare you away from the meadow."

"I had no idea."

"How long do you stay?" he asked, not sure now what he needed to ask and what he should say next. What he was sure of though was that she was a bona fide person, and he was more attracted to her than he had ever thought possible.

"I don't know. I don't know if I even have any control over that. I will stay as long as I possibly can." Amy knew that the meditation was the key, but how to control that was something she had never tried to do before. Until now, this exercise had been a conscious effort on her part to relax and get to sleep. Now she was hoping against all odds that she could stay awake.

"Can I touch you?" he asked hesitantly. She had reached out and touched his arm. The touch felt real. He was convinced now that when he touched her she would be solid and real.

"I hoped with all my heart that you would do that and wondered why you had not already done so," she said it with such tenderness Dan felt as though he might be melting into the meadow. That was all he needed. He reached out and brushed her face with his hand. He had nice hands, strong and weatherworn but gentle. His touch excited Amy beyond anything she had expected. Dan held Amy's face in his hands and looked deep in her eyes.

She felt real; she was real. She couldn't feel that real if she was just his imagination. There was a sensation of overwhelming excitement surging through his body. He suddenly felt emotions that he hadn't thought were possible in a sixty-year-old man. He was as giddy as a school boy on his first date; and in these circumstances, he felt almost as ignorant as he had been as a school boy. The whole experience made him feel quite foolish and out of control.

She felt a gentle warmth flow through her body as his hand swept her cheek. She reached up and touched his hand as it touched her face. It was a simple gesture, and it lit a fire that he was sure now wasn't going to be put out. It was as though their souls met in that touch and locked.

She wanted to touch back. She touched his hand then his arm. She moved closer to him. He moved his body into hers and cradled her as he leaned against the tree. Feeling two arms around her again was just incredible. She felt like her heart and soul had come alive again. When Joe died, she had died inside as well. Now this man had awakened her inner being. Was this crazy or what? She was much too engulfed in emotion by now to be concerned with reality. It was so very quiet and peaceful there in the meadow that she could almost hear the beating of both their hearts in the silence. They were beating together.

"I will be here."

"What?" Amy had heard him correctly but wasn't sure what he meant. She could only hope she understood him, so she asked for reassurance.

"I will be here, waiting, no matter when you come. I will wait for you, Amy."

The alarm was ringing. She could hear the automatic coffee pot brewing in the kitchen. Her canvass was waiting.

CHAPTER 7

Dan Confides in David

Dan awoke the next morning with resolve. He didn't care if Amy was a ghost, a figment of his imagination, or real. He wanted to be with her as much as he could. He was alone there on that big farm and had been satisfied with that since Sue May died. But no longer did he feel that way. He hadn't even felt this way about his wife. He thought he had loved her—he had loved her in his own way—but he had been all about his work, his farming, and himself. He had worked long hours and left her to busy herself around the farm. As much as he loved her, the thought of spending hours sitting around, talking to her, or just holding her would have never appealed to him. Then one day she was gone. Now he found that he wanted to spend every minute he possibly could in the meadow with Amy—a lady who came in and out of his life with no control and stayed but for such temporary moments. However often, however long it was, he would take what he could get. For the first time in sixty years, Dan knew he was deeply in love.

He couldn't infringe on her perfect spot. His intensions were to maintain the appearance of the meadow but somehow be closer so he would not miss her when she came. He chose an area just on the outside of the fence and moved his work shed to that spot. Since Amy had been unable to see the fence, he was sure she would not be able to see the shed either. It took him several days to dismantle and reconstruct the building by himself, but finally he was finished. Now he could see the meadow at all times and continue working while he waited. He tried to finish his farming chores in the mornings or early afternoons so he could be near the meadow in the afternoons. He saved furniture making for those times. His life and his schedule now seemed to revolve around the possibility of being with Amy.

Dan was working on a deacon's bench in front of his newly moved workshop when Jake stopped by to see how he was doing and inquired about the woman who had been in the meadow.

"Wow!" Jake looked surprised. "Did you move that thing all by yourself?"

"Yes, it took me a few days, but I finally got it."

"You should have hollered; I would have helped you move it. Why'd you move it out here in the front yard?"

Dan had not thought of how the shed looked on his property, only that he was able to work and keep a watchful eye for Amy. Now he stepped back and took a hard look. He laughed out loud. "You're certainly right. It adds nothing to the beauty of my place."

Now Jake was curious. Truth be known, he was more curious about what could make Dan laugh out loud than why he moved the shed. In all the years they had been friends, Jake didn't think he had ever heard him laugh audibly. That made him mighty curious.

Dan knew he couldn't tell the truth about moving the shed, so he made up a story about missing visitors who came by. "If I am back behind the barn in this shed working, then people don't think they should bother me; and they just keep going. If I have the shed up front, I can see them. That way, I don't miss anybody's visits."

Of course, Jake didn't believe him for a minute. Most of the time, he knows Dan would just as soon wish people would stay away, but pushing the issue was useless.

"By the way, I asked around town, but no one has heard of anyone new moved into the area. Have you seen the woman out there anymore?"

Dan wasn't a good liar, so he kept working and, without looking up, replied, "Nope, I never saw her again. Whoever she was, she hasn't come back, but thanks for asking around."

He put the last nail in place and stopped to get Jake a cup of coffee. It was almost time for Amy to appear, and he was ready for Jake to go away, but he was also curious to know if Jake would be able to see her. She had been there before when Jake was there, but maybe he just wasn't looking in her direction. This time Dan was going to put it to the test. Just as the conversation lulled and Jake was done with his coffee, Dan saw Amy moving across the meadow.

"Would you look at that? Wild turkeys are in the meadow." Of course, there weren't any turkeys, but he wanted Jake to look that way.

Jake peered beyond the fence but saw nothing. "Where? What turkeys? I don't see any."

"There in the middle of the field now." Dan, by now, was pointing straight at Amy, who was still peacefully strolling across the meadow, unaware of anyone watching her. It was all he could do to control the horrible urge to burst in to peals of laughter.

"I still don't see them." Jake was looking as hard as he could, but he saw nothing.

Dan was extremely relieved that Jake was unable to see Amy, but now he was anxious to go. He hated to miss even a minute that could be spent with her. "Maybe I should go down there and see if I can tell which way they are headed. Turkey dinner sounds pretty good."

Jake shook his head. "I think you just saw some kind of critter. Maybe you need glasses. I gotta be shoving off anyway. I have a couple more stops to make before supper. Thanks for the coffee."

"Thanks for stopping by and for asking around about the newcomer. I don't know what I'd do without you. See you next time."

Dan watched until Jake disappeared down the lane, then he jumped the fence and was halfway across the meadow with one bound.

He was anxious for David to come by. He wanted to tell him about his encounter with the woman in the meadow and explain to him how real she was. He was also interested to see what his brother would make of all this. He was sure he had not convinced his brother that anyone was in the meadow, but someday he would.

He busied himself with one of the benches he had promised Mrs. Colby. She had ordered four of them for her kitchen, and he had been so immersed in watching for Amy that he had forgotten all about getting them finished. Now they were supposed to be ready by Saturday, so he pushed his thoughts aside and got busy on them. At least that would make the time go faster. Now with the workshop located where he had a view of the meadow, he could relax and get his work done.

Dan's wish was granted when he heard David coming down the trail to the farm. He had a cup of coffee and a lot of conversation waiting for him. David had never seen his brother so alive and so anxious to talk. Most of the frown on his face was gone, and his eyes were fairly dancing with excitement. He wasn't sure he really wanted to hear what Dan was going to tell him, but certainly his curiosity about this lady was mounting; and it did make a good tale. Besides, anyone who could make his brother smile couldn't be bad for him.

"Well," David said as he settled on the porch, "you look as though you are bursting at the seams with secrets, and I'm just as anxious to hear what you are to tell. So let's have it, big brother."

"She is so very wonderful, David." Dan was like bubbling oil just about to shoot out of the ground. "I talked to her, I touched her, and I held her in my arms. I don't really understand how she gets here; but believe me, little brother, she is as alive as you and I."

That actually wasn't what David had hoped to hear. He was glad to see his brother so animated and happy; but he wasn't as happy to know that after Dan had confronted the vision, it didn't just dissolve. He had theories about what was going on if Dan was just dreaming up this woman, but none at all if she was really there.

"Did she tell you where she comes from?"

"No, she never mentioned that."

David was curious as to why his brother would not know where she came from if he had talked to her.

"You know, I never thought to ask her."

"Does she come here often?"

"Yes," Dan was talking faster than David could follow as he explained to his brother how Amy happened to come to the meadow and why she always left. David listened intently then let out a long low whistle. "That is some story you are telling. I hope you didn't tell it to very many people."

"No." Dan realized how ridiculous the story sounded. It wasn't even possible. He knew that, and yet there he was involved with the impossible as deeply as he could be. "I would hope that you wouldn't tell anyone either. I understand how strange it all sounds, but I know that it can happen because it has."

"Do you believe love can be strong enough to reach across time or space?"

"I have heard stories about such occurrences, but I always thought they were fairy tales."

"I feel like I am living just such a wonderful adventure, and I love it."

David did not know how to respond to his brother's last remark. His brother, the rational, uninventive one had traded places with him. He was now the one trying to find a rationalization for this whole matter. He was sure there was no explanation. Dan had given him a lot to digest. The concept of a lady who could think herself in and out of a meadow was hard to accept. It was going to take him a few days to digest it all. The strange part was that his rational, logical brother had just accepted this account without reservation and believed with his whole heart that something strange and magical had happened in the meadow. His instant and total acceptance was harder for David to acknowledge than the story he was telling.

He left Dan on the porch, watching for Amy, and headed home. He knew he shouldn't tell anyone, but he needed to talk to Becky about all this. She would have the answer. Of course, once he discussed something with Becky, it would go to Elizabeth, then Mary, then . . . No, he better just figure this one out by himself. If the time was right, he would tell Becky all about it.

CHAPTER 8

The Picture

Amy awoke the next morning not wanting to get out of bed. The sun was streaming in her window; she could hear birds singing outside. What a peaceful feeling she had, and she thought, *Wasn't that just the grandest dream?*

Amy sat straight up in bed and studied the picture hanging on her wall. No, it wasn't a dream, was it? The meadow truly did exist, and the man was real. He had spoken to her. She had spoken to him. This was no man that she had imagined and placed in her meditation spot. Amy had no idea how this was happening, but she knew that something very wonderful and strange was happening to her. Her next thought was to lie back down and try to find the meadow again. *There is so much I want to tell him, and so much I want to ask him.* She wanted to feel the happiness of having him around and being around him and to feel his arms around her again. Even if she went back now, she was sure he would not be there early in the morning. So she got out of bed and started her day.

After that encounter with Dan, Amy began going to the meadow every afternoon. The break in her day and the rest for her aching body was a bonus. Since Dan had shown up, she wasn't going to miss a single day if possible. They would sit under the tree together with his arms around her, share secrets, or watch the brook flow by.

"I promised myself I would never love again. Love can be so painful."

"Do you still feel that way?"

"No, for some strange reason, I don't believe this love is ever going to hurt."

"I promised myself I would never love again too but not for that reason. I don't think I ever wanted to have to adjust my life or my schedule to suit someone else again."

"Do you still feel that way?"

By now, Amy was laughing. "No, my whole schedule now is you."

He made her feel so warm and protected. She had not felt that way since she and Joe had first married. She knew there had to be some great mystery to all of this, but for the moment, she was content to allow it just to be that—a mystery. The magnetism she felt when she was around this man told her this had been more than just a chance meeting. She felt there must have been a very good reason they had been united in the meadow. There had to be some purpose in this union, but she had no idea what it might be. Surely, if he had been someone she had known before, she would have remembered him. What she did know for sure was how content and relaxed she felt when they were together; and as much as she loved this feeling, she hated it as well. Because she knew that the more relaxed she felt with Dan, the closer she was to leaving him.

One afternoon, he asked, "What do you do when you are not here? How do you pass your days?"

"I help my daughter run her store, and I paint whenever I have the time. Occasionally, I even sell a painting. I have painted this lovely meadow and have the painting hanging on my bedroom wall. So even in my waking hours, I can enjoy its beauty and peace."

"If I bring you pencil and paper, could you draw the meadow for me?"

"Certainly." Then she hesitated. "Well, I am not really sure. I don't think I could carry anything like that into the meadow, and I don't know if I can use any tangible thing here either. You could bring me pencil and paper, and I will see if it will work. I would love to do it for you".

"I will try to find whatever you need. Maybe if it is here, you will be able to use it."

By the time Amy returned to the meadow that evening, Dan had put some paper and charcoal pencils under the tree for her. It was interesting that she could not see his fence or house, but here lay the pencils and paper. Amy found the pencil worked smoothly on the paper. It was a nice quality of charcoal, and the drawing became quite a stunning success for just a sketch. She was surprised that she was able to use the pencil and even more amazed that she managed to finish the little sketch without leaving the meadow.

Dan was very pleased with the results and even more pleased that Amy was able to use the drawing material there in the meadow. For a fleeting moment, it had given him hope of something more for them than the meadow. If Amy could use the pencil and paper he had given her, what else could she use?

"I have just the spot to hang this," he said. He was holding the sketch as though it might escape his grasp, and Dan truly was afraid it might. What would keep the sketch from disappearing when Amy did? It was his paper he had brought with him. Surely, it would stay with him.

"It will be my greatest treasure while you are not with me."

"Wait," she said as she reached for the sketch, "I haven't signed it yet." She took the paper and wrote her usual signature on the bottom—her initials and the year: AMB '06.

"Hey, that's not right. You are definitely hurrying time. It is still only 1905."

Such a simple sentence and yet it engulfed the wide space that lay between them. Of course, Amy was too stunned to respond. That was the answer to many of Amy's questions—right there; the answer was so simple. It had been there all the time. Somehow she had gotten herself into a meadow that was not in her time. How?

Amy was now staring at Dan like she had just seen him for the first time. "Dan," she said very hesitantly, for she was not sure how he was going to react to her next statement. "In my world, it is 2006."

He looked astonished; but after a moment of recovery, he realized he was not really surprised. "I knew that you were not from around here. I knew that something was very different about you. I just couldn't figure out how or what it was."

"How could we have missed each other by a hundred and one years?"

Dan grew silent and sad. Interestingly enough, Amy suddenly felt that same sadness. The realization of the situation suddenly had come to them both almost simultaneously.

"This information makes my heart very sad, Amy, for it certainly means that we will never really be together. For the past few weeks, I have been somehow hoping that you had come from just another area; and I would be able to eventually find you and bring you to the meadow in person. My heart and soul belong to you as much as if you lived in my house with me now. I have never loved anyone as I love you or known such happiness as I feel when I am with you. I will take what I can get. I don't know how to get to you, so please come back to me whenever you can. I will always wait, Amy, here in the meadow."

Amy felt Dan's arms tighten around her. She knew all hope of anything, but those fleeting precious moments would never be possible. She too had hoped that somehow she would find Dan and his meadow. Now, it was the moment they must live for.

"Oh, Dan, I will come as often as I can and stay as long as I can. I'm not really sure how I get here either. I don't know why I came here, but I feel the same. I have never felt such peace and fulfillment as I feel when I'm sitting here with you in the circle of your arms, hearing your voice, and feeling you next to me."

The phone was ringing. Amy groaned as she reached for the phone. She must remember from now on to turn off that ringer. It was harsh to be yanked from the meadow to answer a phone.

It was her daughter. That was just as well. It was time Amy told her daughter about all this and what was going on. She was very interested to hear what thoughts she might have on such a thing.

"Yes, lunch is great. I'll meet you at the coffee shop."

Amy sat on the edge of her bed, going over the last meeting she had with Dan. A hundred and one years was a wide time span. They had only moments together, but wasn't life made up of only moments? Don't we all just live it a moment at a time?

She had a lot to think about before lunch.

CHAPTER 9

The Book

Dan was headed down the road to town. He had some woodworking supplies to pick up and some benches to deliver to McDonald's country store. Walking on the road just ahead of him was a man he had never seen around those parts. Strangers didn't show up too often. He stopped alongside him. The man was of medium built, thin brown hair that hung to his shoulders, and piercing blue eyes. Dan felt the hairs on the back of his neck standing up. The man on the road didn't really look dangerous. Still, he gave Dan a very strange feeling that didn't go away.

"Say, if you are headed to town, I can give you a ride as far as the country store. I'm on my way there to deliver these benches."

"Thank you." The stranger climbed up on the seat beside Dan. "I am on my way to Charlotte. I have written a book, and I am going there to try and get it published."

"Well, I'm not going that far, but I'll give you a ride as far as I'm going." Dan grew increasingly uncomfortable as they rode along in silence. "What's your book about? Dan had never really cared much for reading and had little interest in books, but he felt the need to make small talk to ease the strained silence.

"It is a collection of stories concerning misplaced lovers and their ability to reconnect with one another."

Now Dan was no longer making small talk. He was very interested. "Do you believe that is possible?"

"Definitely, I do. I have recorded several of those occurrences in my book. I believe you would be very fascinated by them."

Dan looked directly at him. He sensed this stranger knew something about Amy and about their meeting. Surely, that could not be possible. Now the man was looking straight into Dan's eyes. "Are you not interested in time travel yourself?"

"Yes, I am. How did you know that?"

"I just know those things."

"Have you experienced time travel yourself?"

"If I answered yes, would you believe me?"

By now, Dan was intently focused on the odd little man. "I think you already know the answer to that question."

They had reached McDonald's, and Dan was relieved that the ride was over. He had never been particularly social, and this conversation had made him terribly uncomfortable. He jumped out and started unloading the first bench.

"Say," he hollered over his shoulder, "if you get that book published, let me know. I would like to buy a copy and read it."

There was no response. When he looked up, the man was nowhere in sight. He looked up and down the road as far as he could see, but the strange man had just vanished. Then Dan saw it. The man had left the book on the wagon seat.

He picked up the book. It was small, and holding it made his hands tingle. United Souls Through the Ages was printed in gold letters on the front. This would be one book Dan would read. He tucked it in his back pocket and hauled the benches inside the store.

Before meeting her daughter at the coffee shop, Amy had enough time to stop in the bookstore next to her daughter's shop. She was looking for something—anything—that might tell her about time travel. Maybe somewhere, there was a connection between meditation and time. She secretly hoped that she would just find a book that somehow might explain what was going on.

The little book store was nestled in among several small unique shops. The small shopping mall contained only specialty shops, one of which belonged to her daughter. There was also an art studio, where local artists sold their painting, and a nice coffee shop, where she and Nikki often had lunch or coffee. A few of Amy's paintings were on display in the studio, and she was hoping to have a few new ones there by next week.

The book nook had always been one of Amy's favorite spots. It was small and crowded with all sorts of literature and music. She often stopped in here on her way to her daughter's shop. Today there was a different smell and feel to the shop. Amy wasn't sure what the difference was. Everything still looked the same, but there was a damp, musty smell about the place similar to an old attic or a basement. There was a new clerk today too. She often stopped in this little book nook, but she had never seen him before. He was old. Amy couldn't be sure how old, but she was sure he should have been retired. He looked to have been just average size but now was stooped and gray. His hair was thin and almost shoulder length. He had a long thin nose and yellowed teeth. His clothes had a worn-out and lived-in appearance. His eyes were bright blue; and when he looked at her, she felt as though he could see within her very soul. Something about him was very peculiar; something Amy just couldn't put her finger on. As he approached her, she had an uncomfortable feeling.

"Lets see," he said, "I can usually guess what a customer has come looking for. I've been working in bookstores for many years now, and I have seen them all. I believe you are interested in time travel, correct?" Amy felt a strange sensation creep up her spine.

How would this odd little man know something like that? Who was he? He looked almost a century old, but his voice was strong and unfaltering.

"Why, yes," she said. Trying to appear matter-of-fact, she added, "That is exactly what I came looking for. How did you know that?"

"Just a feeling, I have an insight for these things." And as he smiled, Amy felt as though he knew all about Dan and her visits to the meadow.

She looked at him more closely. Perhaps this odd little man could explain what was happening to her. "Do you believe in time travel?" she asked, not really expecting an answer.

There was a long pause. Then, very quietly he said, "Philip J. Bailey wrote, 'We live in deeds, not years; in thoughts, not breaths; in feelings, not in figures on a dial. We should count time by heart throbs.' I believe that I agree with him. If you are asking me if I believe one can move through space and time, then my answer is definitely yes. I believe that certain people were made to be together and that wherever or whenever they are, one's soul will always be seeking the other."

Amy made no response. This man whom she had never met had voiced in two sentences what she had spent paragraphs putting together in her mind. She was about to ask him if he had ever had such an experience himself when he interrupted her thoughts.

"There have been others who have had similar experiences. Perhaps you would be interested in reading about them."

He handed Amy what appeared to be a very old book entitled, *United Souls Through the Ages*. It was a small book, and it had a musty smell to it as though it had been stored in an attic for years. The edges were still gilded, and there were no frays on the cover. Odd; a book that old should have tattered corners at least.

Amy thanked him. When she opened her purse to pay for the book, he raised a hand. "No," he said, "this is a gift from me to you. Please enjoy it." Amy didn't know why this man should be giving her a gift, but the whole experience was so out of the ordinary that she just walked out of the bookstore deep in thought without any argument. She was sure that the man in the bookstore somehow was there just to give her this book. What she didn't know was where he came from or who he was.

She started next door to meet her daughter at the coffee shop, when suddenly she remembered that she had set down her purse to pay the man while they were talking, and she must have left it sitting there. She turned to go back in for it.

As she came back in to the shop, she was aware that the musty aroma was gone; and the bookstore appeared to be back to normal. She noticed a young woman coming from the back room. She remembered this clerk from some of her visits as not being particularly pleasant or helpful, but she was looking especially bedraggled and annoyed today.

"Excuse me," Amy said as pleasantly as possible, "I was so engrossed in my conversation with your other clerk that I walked out and left my purse sitting here.

Yes, here it is. I was just going to put it in the lost and found."

Amy had seen the purse immediately, sitting just where she had left it. As she picked it up, she asked, "Would you ask him to come out front please? I wanted to thank him for the book. I was so interested in it that I walked out without thanking him. He was so very helpful."

"What man? What other clerk? There isn't anyone else on the schedule here today but me. I'm pretty miffed about it. I was supposed to get some relief at 2:00 this afternoon, but the schedule shows no one but me; so I guess I'm here alone till closing tonight. I have told them and told them I can't stay that long, but they don't pay any attention to me."

"There was an older man working here just a few minutes ago. He gave me this book and wouldn't let me pay for it."

The clerk took the book from Amy, examined it, and then returned it.

"I know just about every book in here, and I am sure that one didn't come from this store. I have never heard of it or seen it before."

"It has to have come from here. See, here is my purse I left. I was just here talking to the other clerk."

"I don't think we have ever had a man working here. As long as I have been here, it has only been female clerks. I don't know who you were talking to, but it wasn't another clerk."

Amy realized it was senseless to argue with her. She also knew the girl was probably right. This was just one more incidents in a long string of unbelievable incidents that had been happening to her lately. She opted for a polite but hurried exit. "Thank you for saving my purse," said Amy on her way out the door.

A feeling of something she couldn't put a name to was creeping into her mind. By now, her life seemed anything but ordinary. She had grown to think of herself as a little old lady who would peacefully live out her retirement years in a nice spot with her family with no serious worries or cares. Nothing unusual—she would just sleep, eat, paint, and live the good life.

Now suddenly, she somehow seemed to be moving through time and space and had attached herself to some wonderfully tender human being in some other time and place. She had no idea why this was happening to her or how it was happening. All she could do was hope that she could continue to get back to the meadow until she got this all sorted out in her mind.

CHAPTER 10

Amy Confides in Nikki

Amy had not discussed what had happened with her daughter yet. She couldn't be sure how Nikki would react. She also had not been quite ready to share her experience. There had been no way to answer the questions that were bound to come. Amy had no answers for herself, let alone her daughter; but now with the discovery of the hundred and one year's difference in time, she was ready to hear what her daughter could make of it all.

Nikki was waiting when she arrived at the coffee shop. She had ordered coffee and sandwiches, so at least that was one decision Amy didn't have to make. She was beginning to feel like she couldn't make another decision ever again. Her daughter had always been her best friend, and they shared many secrets; but she hated to sound like a lonely, foolish, old woman who had invented some man to fantasize about. If her daughter thought that were true, she would be busy matching her with some of the older men she knew. Amy certainly didn't want that.

"You're late," Nikki said as her mom came hurrying up. "And you have a very strange look on your face. What is going on?" "I just met a very weird man in the bookstore, who was supposed to be working there, and then he wasn't working there."

Nikki's face had a look that said, *What on earth are you talking about?* even though she hadn't gotten the question out of her mouth yet.

"Maybe I better start from the beginning, and that will help clear up the last statement." Amy laughed, knowing how strange that must have sounded. She picked up her sandwich and took a bite.

"I just realized I haven't eaten yet today. So much has happened that I forgot. Did I ever tell you about my meditation place that I created?"

"No, but I knew you meditated."

"It's a beautiful, peaceful meadow with a grand old shade tree and a babbling brook running through it. I have always used it in the meditation exercise Susie started me with years ago."

"I have seen the beautiful picture of a meadow in your bedroom. Is that the one?"

"Yes, that is the one. I go there in my mind when I lie down at night, and it helps me relax and get to sleep. Since I moved here, I have been lying down in the afternoons. I never used to do that, but it seemed to help ease my back pain. Suddenly one afternoon, there was a man in the meadow."

"A man? What kind of a man?" Nikki understood about the meadow so far, but the introduction of a man had her stumped. "I don't know what man. He just appeared one afternoon."

"What does he do in your meadow?"

"The first time I saw him, he simply sat down under the tree with me and said nothing. I remember thinking how nice it was to actually have some company. I was sure that I have just conjured him up for that reason. How else could I explain the presence of a man in my imaginary spot?"

"Does he come often?"

"Yes, now he is there almost every time I am."

"What does he look like? Is he someone you might have once known?"

"He is very nice-looking, and no, I have never seen him before nor does he look like anyone I ever knew."

"Do you think you created him because you are alone, Mom?" Nikki was worried about her mother, and it showed in the tone of her voice. "I have many associates who are close to your age and alone themselves. I could keep your social schedule very busy. Let me set something up for tonight."

"No, honestly I'm not really lonely. Maybe at first, after your father died, I was feeling a little abandoned; but since I moved here, I love my small house, and working in your shop gives me plenty of company. I actually enjoy being by myself with time to paint. It isn't that, I am sure."

"Well, at least an imaginary man can't break your heart or do you any physical harm." Nikki laughed at the thought of having a man you could make do anything you wanted to.

"Actually, that is the problem. He isn't imaginary; you see, he is a real, living, breathing man, Nikki. He has a name. It is Dan Kerr. He puts his arms around me and sits under the tree with me in quiet peacefulness. We trade secrets and dreams. I have been going as often to the meadow as I can manage to get there.

"No need to look at me that way. I am very aware that I sound crazy. Do you believe in time travel?"

"Truthfully, mom, I have always had a fascination for that subject."

"Apparently, this man is living now in 1905. He actually owns a meadow that looks exactly like the one I envisioned. He has lived alone for the last twenty years. We would probably have never found each other if I had not started going to the meadow in the afternoons. Somehow he happened to see me there; and now not only can he see me, but he can talk to me and touch me. I know, I'm just a crazy old lady with a vivid imagination, right?"

Nikki realized that her mother was sincere about what she was saying, and somehow she believed this might actually be happening. Her mother had always been great at meditation. She had always had a special knack for clearing her mind and receiving messages. Nikki herself had often asked her mother to meditate on such things as her job moves or her love to see what vibrations she felt. Love and time travel had always been one of Nikki's favorite subjects as well, and she was convinced that it was possible. She was sure that everyone had a soul mate whether in their time or someone else's and that somehow it was possible for you to meet no matter what circumstances separated you. It didn't take her long to recover from her mother's announcement of the imaginary man.

"I don't think it is your imagination, Mom. You have never been one who would create something like this. I know you miss Dad, but I hardly think as busy as you are with your painting and your life here that you would be that lonely. Besides, you have me as well, and I would be there for you anytime you felt you needed someone.

"I do have a wonderful imagination," Amy admitted, "but I am sure this is something far from that. The emotions I feel tell me so. I don't think I really loved your father like I love this man. From the moment I saw him, I felt as though I belonged to him somehow. That was how I knew he had to be real. No one could feel that kind of a bond to an imaginary figure. I don't know if we somehow knew each other in another life or were supposed to have known each other. I haven't yet put all the pieces together."

"I think all of this is quite exciting, and I am happy for you; but I am going to need some time to adjust to all this."

"I need you to think hard about this for me. I desperately want to know what you think I should do about it all."

"I will do that, Mom. Give me a day or two to think it over, and maybe I can help you figure out how it happened."

"So what is the deal with the man in the bookstore?"

Amy told her daughter all about the strange encounter with the odd little man and how he had given her the book and refused to let her pay. She produced the musty old book that the gentleman had given her. "I haven't had a chance to read it yet, but I'm sure it applies to the type of thing that is happening to me. I went back to thank him for the book, but he was gone. They said no man worked there, but he was there; and he gave me this book. I'll examine it tonight, and then I will pass it on to you; and you can do the same."

"What are you going to do about Dan?"

"I don't know what I'm going to do about Dan. That is what you are supposed to tell me. I realize that we can never really be together, but I miss him when we are apart. I don't know what is going to happen to us. I guess I will just continue to go to the meadow as often as possible and hope that he is always there. What would you do?" "Right now, I have no idea what I would do. It is certainly a dilemma.""Do you have any idea where he is located?"

"Apparently, he is somewhere here in North Carolina. He said he was somewhere north of Charlotte."

"Maybe that is the answer. Maybe you never found him before because you were in the wrong state or still the wrong time or the wrong time of day. I don't know that answer. Have you considered going through the records downtown at the courthouse to see if you could locate the farm or find what happened to him? Often, you can harvest information like that over the Internet."

"No, this is all so new that I haven't really taken time to rationalize it all. I guess the truth is I was just enjoying him, so I didn't want to find out anything that would make him disappear. You are right. I should find out if he was ever a real person. That shouldn't be too hard."

"Please keep me posted, Mom. I would like to know who he is too. If you need any help in the search, let me know. I will be glad to try my luck."

Even though Nikki had always been supportive of her mother, she had not been totally convinced that her mother wasn't imagining things; and she was more than a little concerned. She had always loved the idea of time travel, but it had always just been in a movie or a book. Never would she have dreamed that her mother could be involved in such a fantasy. She made a mental note to herself to try and take her mom to lunch more often.

CHAPTER 11

The Investigation

Amy settled into a comfortable spot with some time on her hands and a desire to examine the book she had been given today by the strange little man. She turned it slowly over and over in her hands. It was a small book—not much more than four inches wide and six inches tall. It had an unusual smell to it. There was a hint of incense, mustiness, and outdoors. The outside cover was in nice condition. The gilding on the edges of the book was still in perfect shape. Yet the smell and the pages themselves told Amy this book was very, very old. The front page gave only a title: *United Souls Through the Ages*. There was no publishing company, no date, and no copyright. There was only a text. Amy began to read.

The first text page contained a poem by John Burroughs. Amy read and reread the last verse. "Nor time, nor space, nor deep, nor high can keep my own away from me." It set the theme for the entire book.

> The stars come nightly to the sky;
> The tidal wave unto the sea;
> Nor time, nor space, nor deep, nor high
> Can keep my own away from me

The little book contained stories of lovers united through time and space—stories Amy had never read or head about. They made her spine tingle, for she knew her story should be written on these pages as well. What a special gift, this little book. She would pass it on to her daughter as well. Nikki would love reading these strange stories.

It didn't explain why this was happening to her, but it did give her some comfort that others had experienced similar situations. The only explanation she could come up with was one of location. She had never lived in North Carolina before, and she had not seen Dan before she moved here. According to him, the meadow was somewhere not far from Charlotte, so that would explain part of it. Maybe also the time of day had caused this. She never used to go to the meadow except at night. Amy also realized that for her the meadow was always warm, sunny, and dry. Surely, if there was a real place such as this, it would get dark at night. The darkness may have hidden her presence from him until now.

Maybe it was all making more sense. The one thing that didn't really make sense was, why her? She had always felt a great deal of love for her husband, and she was sure Dan had felt the same for his wife. Of course, she had never seen Dan in her meadow before Joe died. The location, the light, and Joe's death—the combination had to be the key. All of the stories had some trigger that had made them happen and some logical reason behind them. Her story must be the same. Maybe if she could find out more about Dan and his family, she would find the key. Maybe the key was still out in there somewhere in her future. How could they have been meant for each other? It was time to investigate further.

Amy had searched and searched most of the night for the records that might tell her who Dan was and where he was. Never was a computer whiz, she thought perhaps she was just not typing in the right questions for try as she might, there was no information on Dan Kerr. She had gone to dozens of sites and read hundreds of facts about people named Dan Kerr, but none of them was the right Dan Kerr.

"Nikki?"

"Hi, Mom, what are you doing up so early?"

"I was up most of the night on the computer, trying to gain information about anyone named Dan Kerr in or around this area, but I have done nothing but strike out."

"Go down to the city county building and check with the county clerk. They should have all the local information you would ever need."

"Of course, I will go now. They should be open. Wish me luck. I'll call as soon as I find out anything at all."

"Thanks, Mom. If I have any time today, I will try my luck at searching on the computer myself for you. How did you spell his last name again?"

"K-e-r-r."

"OK. Good luck downtown."

The local county building was her next step. They usually had all sorts of records. Amy got to the courthouse so early there was no one to help her. A security guard did manage to direct her to the county clerk's office. Luckily, no one was there yet except for the clerk. She was sitting behind a huge stack of files and typing furiously on a computer keyboard.

"Excuse me, I'm from Ohio and only recently moved here, but I have some distant relatives who lived here; and I am trying to locate them." Amy certainly wasn't going to tell this girl she was searching for a strange man in a meadow. The relative story sounded better.

"Where did they live?"

"I'm not sure, but I believe they owned a farm somewhere just north of Charlotte. I would like to know if I could possibly find any information on them in here."

The clerk was mildly annoyed by her request. "I don't have time to go through all those records for you, I'm sorry. We are in the process of putting all of our files on the computer, and I am expected to work and enter this whole stack of files today."

"Would it be possible for me to dig for the information myself?"

"Certainly." The clerk brightened up. "You will find it more than a little overwhelming, I'm afraid." She led Amy to another room piled high with boxes and boxes of old records.

"We are in the process of trying to computerize all of this. I'm afraid they are in a terrible mess, but please feel free to go through any of them you would like. The city files are on the left, the county files on the right. Good luck." The clerk closed the door and left Amy to her task.

By midafternoon, Amy had no more information than she had started with. Her back was aching, and her eyes were burning from reading so many files. She had found four farms owned by people with the same last name but no Dan Kerr. Those four farms had apparently been sold off and developed into housing developments as Charlotte had grown. She had traced them all back finally to 1908 but could find nothing past there.

She closed up the last file and headed out.

"Did you find what you needed?" The clerk, at least, sounded hopeful.

"No, thank you very much for all your help though. There doesn't seem to be any information for the years before 1908."

"Oh, I am so sorry. I should have thought to ask you how far back you wanted to go."

"Why is that?"

"The old courthouse burned to the ground in 1907. All the records were destroyed. If what you need is before that, I'm afraid no one can be of much help. That is the reason we are trying to get all the records on the computer now so they will never be lost again that way."

There it was. The dead end Amy had feared. She took the information about the four farms and headed for her car. She flipped open her cell phone as she walked to the car.

"Nikki?"

"Hi, Mom."

"What are you doing?"

"Working on the store books."

"Can you take a break? I am on my way to an adventure and would sure love some company."

"Sure!" Nikki was always up for an adventure, and besides, she was tired of working. "What time are we going?"

"Grab your purse. I'm almost at your front door."

"Where are we going?" It was more suspense than Nikki could stand.

"Northern Charlotte, looking for a lost farm." As they rode, Amy explained how she had gathered what little information she could; and now, the only thing left was to drive the countryside around Charlotte, looking for the plots she believed could have been the farm.

What they found was that most of the land listed as farms on the old records was now shopping malls or residential areas. Charlotte had spread in all directions as it grew, and any farm very close to town would have been long since swallowed up by civilization. It was a disappointing drive.

"We will keep looking. Somewhere there has to be a record of Dan and his farm."

"We could call every Kerr in the phone book and ask them if they had a relative named Dan."

Amy laughed out loud at that one. How funny. "I don't think I truly care if I ever find the records. We have such a short time together, and I enjoy it so; I would not want to jeopardize that for anything."

The last plot had an interstate highway going though it. Just on the other side of the interstate was an enchanting old barn. Funny, she had not found that one before in her search. She stopped to take several pictures of it. The vines climbed to the top of it and sprouted forth their blooms. There was a wooded area just behind it and what appeared to be more housing developments on the other side of that. At least Amy had found this beautiful barn. She was very attracted to it. She took pictures from several different angles and headed home. She wanted to get to the meadow in time to see Dan.

CHAPTER 12

The Portrait

Amy was a landscape artist. She loved fields, streams, and old barns. Portraits had always been beyond her grasp, but the only way to hold on to Dan was to put him on canvass. Amy worked on a sketch of Dan. She never liked doing faces because she had never been good at it. The picture wasn't going as well as she had hoped; still, it did resemble him. She wasn't very pleased with it, but it looked enough like him that she knew who it was. Painting a face was difficult enough when you had a person or a picture to draw from. With no picture to work from, she had to just picture him in her mind and try to recreate him from that image. Once she had finished, it was off to the frame shop. The finished product wasn't stunning, but Amy was satisfied with it. She wished she could show it to him.

Her life stayed on track in 2006. She continued working at her daughter's shop. She continued painting barns, flowers, and birds and managed to even sell enough to keep her busier than she wanted to be. Her days seemed routine and normal. For all outside appearances, she was a sweet, normal little old lady until she lay down in her bed.

The truth was, of course, that Amy's life was anything but normal. There was nothing normal or ordinary about meeting a man from the year 1905 in an imaginary meadow during meditation sessions. There was nothing ordinary about being deeply in love with someone she could never have. There was absolutely nothing ordinary about spanning time and space on a daily basis.

Amy had just finished the little book she had been given by the man in the bookstore. She thought she might put Dan's mind at ease by informing him of others who had similar experiences. "You know we are not the only ones this has happened to."

"No, I have read a book that has documented several cases very similar to ours."

Amy looked at Dan and a strange feeling began to creep over her. "Where did you read that?"

"Interesting you should ask. That was a peculiar thing. There was a man who I had never seen around here before. I gave him a ride one afternoon, and he left a book on my wagon seat."

"Is it a small brown book?"

"Yes, how did you know that?"

What did he look like?"

"Medium build, long brown hair—"

Amy was starting to see a pattern to all this. She interrupted Dan. "Did he make you feel strange?"

"Why, yes, how did you know that?"

"I think I met the same man; only he had gray hair; and he gave me the same book. Who do you think he was?"

"I don't know, but he was apparently able to move through time with more ease than we can. The book helped me to understand that we are not alone or even unique."

"We may never know who he was, but I think he may have been one of the cases in the book. Do you think he could be searching for a lost love?"

"I had not thought of that, but I know he certainly made me uncomfortable."

Amy never really wanted to delve into the details surrounding her and Dan. It was enough for her to just be able to meet him. The whys and the hows had never really troubled her. It fascinated Amy to know she was able to speak to Dan that he could also speak to her. She was able to touch him, to feel his arms around her, and to feel his breath on her neck. She felt that she could tell him anything. She confided in him all the secrets of her soul.

He would always laugh with each secret and say, "Why, Ms. Amy, should you be telling a strange man such deep dark thoughts?"

"No, I certainly shouldn't, but I rather enjoy doing it anyway."

"I rather enjoy hearing them too."

Amy realized that she had never actually told Joe how she felt about a lot of things. Some things you just didn't talk about, and some things you just didn't feel important enough to talk about when your partner was always in a hurry and had little time for you. Many of her thoughts and ideas had just stayed within her—unacknowledged and unspoken until now.

Dan loved hearing Amy talk. She laughed easily, and she made him feel as though he was the only thing in the world that made any difference to her. He listened to her secrets, and he told her his. It was so right—this sharing of secrets. The two of them had nothing but this time together in the meadow. They were not going to hurry through a single moment they might manage to spend together.

He was always amazed at the things she would tell and loved every one of them. He never had a woman tell him many of the things she would say. He never thought the things she would say were foolish or harsh, right or wrong. He just enjoyed hearing them. He returned them with secret thoughts of his own. He had never talked to anyone, let alone a woman as he was talking to Amy, or she to any other man as she talked to him. There seemed to be no boundaries and no fear of hurt or loss of pride at any thought or idea. They told of family, of friends, of experiences, of fears, and of concerns. They spent what seemed like hours telling each other about their lives and their deepest secrets, interlocking their souls to their very depths. Yet Amy knew it couldn't be hours, for she realized her time in the meadow could not have been very long. She never knew how long she could maintain her position in the meadow or when she would leave it for sleep.

Dan had loved his first wife—at least he had considered it to be love. He had worked hard to provide for her and to make her life as easy as possible. He now realized that he had been so busy working hard to give her a nice home that he had forgotten to give her the most important thing—himself. She was his partner, his cook, and his roommate; and when she was gone, he mourned her and missed her. Even in all of that, he now realized that she had never been his soul mate. They had never shared secrets or bared their hearts and minds to each other. What a blessing that he could at last understand what love really should be. Maybe in this world, there truly was only one person who could be your soul mate and maybe who wasn't always in your same time frame. Whatever the explanation, Dan had no doubt that this lovely lady in the meadow was the center of his universe. He only wished with all his heart that they had more time together. He had never felt the kind of love for his wife, who he lived with for twenty years like the love he felt for Amy, who he saw in so few fleeting moments.

Dan longed for more time with Amy for another reason as well. Lately, the dizzy spells had been coming more and more often and lasting longer and longer. It was the one secret he would never tell her. They had so few precious moments together. He was not going to interject any form of concern into them. He would simply be in the meadow with Amy as long as possible.

CHAPTER 13

The Revelation

Dan realized that Amy's meadow must always be sunny, warm, and bright. Day or night, she would move through the meadow with the same ease and direction. She seemed unaware of the elements or the light. For Dan, the meadow was not always so pleasant. It rained there; it grew dark there. When fall came, it would also grow cold. Dan didn't know how much longer Amy would come to the meadow, but he was going to try making life easier there for himself. Often, Amy came very late at night; and with no moon, it was very difficult to know if she was there or not.

Unsure of whether he could construct anything in the meadow without changing everything else, he took a chance. He went well above his head on the old oak and constructed a rooflike structure which covered the area under the tree where he and Amy sat. Next, he built some freestanding walls behind the tree at an angle to help keep off wind and other elements. He bought some extra lanterns and hung them from the walls. He would light them in the evening, and hopefully, she would come before they burned out. Dan was relieved that the meadow was well hidden from the road. What would the neighbors think if they saw him out there building what seemed to be a lean-to around the tree? Several of his friends in town were already worried enough about him being out there on the farm alone.

Their concerns were warranted. The one secret that Dan had never shared with Amy was a heart condition, which had been discovered when he was a child.

"It's some type of malformation in his heart," the doctor had announced after a lengthy examination.

"What caused it?" Dan's mother was gravely concerned.

"We are not sure. It could cause him immediate trouble, or he could live with this for years."

"He is only seven. How long do you think he has?" He remembered hearing the worry in his mother's voice. He didn't really understand at all because he didn't feel a bit sick. He didn't really understand what they were talking about.

"Guess there is no way to predict that; only time will tell."

Now Dan was sixty and still going. Most of the time, it was no problem, but once in a while, the fluttering and dizziness made him very aware that his days were numbered.

Neighbors would drop by from time to time just to check on him. He had always welcomed them gratefully and appreciated their concerns and had enjoyed having the company, but now he was hoping they would all just stay away.

Amy had been doing some serious thinking about all that had happened to her. It was not Dan who was out of his element; she was. How had she gotten into his world? Was there a way to get out of the meadow? She was convinced that her confines would remain within the meadow, but should she try to move from there? What would happen if she did? She had never been able to see his home from the meadow even though he often spoke of it as being right over there or up the hill. Apparently, it was visible to him; but certainly, she had never seen a sign of it. No man could be expected to live in a meadow. Is it possible that he could add anything in the meadow, and it sill be her meditation spot? What if he put something there and caused her mind to divert from that spot. Thousands of questions swirled in her head; none of which seemed to have answers. It was more than possible that even if he built something in the meadow, she would not see it.

They were both right. Dan finished his construction and said nothing about it to Amy. He wasn't trying to keep a secret from her, but he was curious to find out if she would actually be able to see it.

The next afternoon, Amy arrived.

"I built a roof in this old tree so we wouldn't get rained on out here."

Amy looked up. "Really?" She had never known Dan to not be truthful, but she saw no roof.

"I put up some wind shields as well behind the tree."

Amy turned to see behind the tree. All she saw was green meadow. "That is interesting because I don't see those either."

They had both felt sure that would happen. As strong as their love was and as much happiness as it gave them both, there was also a strong current of sadness for the time and space between them.

Amy had always been a confident woman. She was sure of her ability as an artist. She was sure of her ability as a wife and mother. Since Dan had shown up, she had nothing but doubts about a large chunk of her life. There were so many unanswered questions that she simply chose to ignore them all and live for the moment. Her daughter had been convinced Dan was real, and Amy wasn't crazy. That was a big hurdle.

Dan had convinced his brother that he wasn't crazy either. Although David was sure there was some lady from somewhere, he wasn't really accepting the idea that she had come from the future. He had seen the sketch that Amy did and accepted that the lady in the meadow had done it, but that didn't mean she was from the future. What could he do to make David understand?

One afternoon, he told Amy about his brother's doubts and how he had convinced him that she was there, but he never believed she could have been from the future. "I think he still believes you are just a neighbor from somewhere we haven't met. I guess it isn't necessary for me to convince him. Whatever he believes won't change our relationship. Still, it would be fun to make a believer out of him."

"I could try to bring something with me—something that could have come from nowhere but the future. I have never brought a tangible object to the meadow. My physical body doesn't actually come here."

"I understand that. It was just an entertaining idea to show David a 2006 newspaper or magazine. That would make him a believer for sure, not to mention the fun I would have seeing the expression on his face when he saw it."

That idea appealed to Amy. She had always loved a challenge as well as a good joke.

"Let me look around tomorrow and see what might help then I will keep trying until hopefully I get here with an item. You are right; that would be fun."

"Before you came, I never thought much in life was exciting; and certainly, nothing was funny. Now I find myself going through my day with assorted amusing ideas floating in my head. That idea of something tangible from the future was my latest amusing thought."

"Does it bother you that he hasn't accepted your account?"

"No, not really, but I would like to hand him some proof."

"I suppose it would be a very hard concept to believe, especially when you had never seen the person in question."

"David and I have always been so close. I guess I just assumed he would accept anything his big brother told him as factual."

At home, Amy phoned Nikki. She would have a good suggestion about what Amy should take. She always had great ideas.

"Good morning," Amy sang into the phone as Nikki's voice came on the line.

"Gracious, you sound cheerful for so early in the morning."

"I have a little problem for you to solve. You are going to love this one." Nikki always loved being the solution. From the tone of her mother's voice, she was sure this was going to be interesting. "OK, shoot, I'm in the thinking mode."

"Dan wanted to prove to his brother that I come from the year 2006. I wanted to try to take something to the meadow with me with today's date on it. He thought maybe a newspaper, but I don't know if I could manage to get all that through time and space."

Nikki's response was almost immediate. "A penny—no, wait, I think one of our new nickels. They are definitely unique-looking these days."

"Oh, what a great idea. I knew you would know what to try."

"Thanks, Nikki. I'll let you know when I get there with it."

"You're welcome, Mom. Good luck."

A nickel—a shiny new 2006 nickel should be just what Dan could use. Pennies were nice, but they still looked the same except for the date. The nickel had changed so much. That would be easy to carry; and if anything would convince David, that would. She had to try. She would just hold tight to the nickel every time she tried to come to the meadow. Maybe, just maybe, eventually the nickel would come with her. So for the next week, every time Amy lay down to meditate, she held fast to the nickel. Sometimes she would hold the nickel in her left hand, sometimes her right. Several times, she held a nickel in both hands but no luck. It was discouraging, but Amy was not one to give up easily. She believed with all her heart that she could do this if she just kept trying. Finally, one afternoon she found herself in the meadow, and clutched tightly in her fist was the nickel.

"Oh, Dan, look!" she exclaimed. She was quite pleased with herself and was smiling her biggest smile. "This should make a believer out of your brother. This is what I chose to bring." She handing him the nickel.

Dan took the small item from her. He realized it was a coin, but he had never seen any that looked like this one. It resembled his nickels. He checked the date and let out a low whistle. Truthfully, he had never been sure he really believed Amy was from the future either until that moment. He experienced a moment of sadness once again. It was the same sadness he had felt when Amy had told him she was from the year 2006. The nickel was simply tangible proof that he and Amy would always be separated. Still, the thought of seeing David's face when he handed him that nickel seemed to ease the pain. He put it in his pocket. He was ready now for David next time he came, but right now, the most important thing to Dan was holding on to Amy.

David's weekly visits had become more frequent. He was concerned about his brother's health, but more than his body, he was concerned about his mind. The two men would sit out on the porch—sip coffee and try to analyze what was happening. He had never said anything not even to his wife about this strange occurrence. Those things have a way of getting around—even the best kept secrets, and he didn't want the whole community thinking his brother had gone off the deep end out there in the woods alone. He had wanted to talk this whole thing over with Becky so many times, but he knew it was just too interesting for her not to discuss with some of her friends. He couldn't do that to his brother, so he wisely kept his own council. Some of the people in town were already talking about what might be going on out here. He had tried to put out the fires of talk but with no luck. He certainly wasn't going to add fuel to the fire.

David never believed that the lady came from another time. He had two theories: one, she was a ghost that his brother was seeing; or two, she was a neighbor who Dan really had never met just playing games with him. He had offered both of these theories often, but Dan was insistent that neither of them were right.

So it happened as they were sitting on the porch late one afternoon, talking over the situation as they always did. Lately the mysterious lady and her comings and goings had been the only topic of conversation. Dan seemed to be able to talk of nothing else, and David was determined to convince him he was wrong about the time travel theory.

Suddenly, Dan remembered what he had been waiting all week to give his little brother—the proof he had been looking for. He reached in his pocket and handed David something small.

"What's this?"

"Well, maybe you better just take a look and tell me."

Dan was smiling like David had never seen his brother smile. This man who was born with a frown and never lost it was grinning from ear to ear. Something was going on to bring an expression like that to Dan's face.

"Amy brought it with her yesterday afternoon. She has been trying for a week to get here with it, and finally yesterday, it came with her."

David's face took on a strange expression. He became just slightly pale and stopped talking completely. He turned the coin over and over in his hands. Where could his brother possibly have gotten such a thing if not from the lady? There it was—a small thing, but it made a very loud statement. For in his hand he held a United States minted nickel with the date clearly printed on it—2006.

David, at last, had been convinced that Dan was right. "There isn't any way you could have made this up. I am a believer, big brother. I will never doubt you again." He had finally gotten his voice back.

"It's OK. I know it had to be a hard concept to accept. I'm not sure I did myself until Amy brought that coin."

"I don't really want anyone else to know about this."

"No, I don't think I would either."

"Since Jake started asking around for information, the whole community has started talking. This would bring them all out here, and I might never see Amy again."

"I would never betray your confidence, big brother."

"I knew that. I just wanted to tell you how I felt."

Dan noticed that his brother's gaze had gone to the meadow; and if he could have gotten paler, he would have. Dan's back was to the meadow, but he was sure what had happened. Amy must have come walking through. He didn't know if anyone else would have ever been able to see her or not. Strange that his brother could see her now, for she had come before when David was there; but he never saw her. The coin must have been the connection.

He said nothing, waiting for David to say something. Finally, his mouth opened to say something; but nothing came out.

Dan laughed out loud. "Cat got your tongue, little brother? Didn't you ever see a ghost before?"

Looking over his shoulder, he saw Amy making her usual stroll across the meadow. He wanted more than anything to run to her, but he wasn't taking David to the meadow; and he hated to leave him sitting alone on the porch. One person in Amy's meadow was probably more than enough.

David finally caught his breath and whistled a long low note. "Wow, I knew you weren't crazy, brother; but I never really thought there was a lady either. I just didn't know what was going on. Look how content and happy she appears to be. No wonder you love to watch her there. The world could use that peacefulness if we could just pass it around."

"Well, I never thought you would be able to see her; but it's wonderful that you have. At least, you realize that I have actually been seeing someone; and she is truly wonderful. She makes my life feel complete. Even when I'm here all alone, I don't feel alone. I don't know how or why this happened, but I am certainly blessed that it did."

"I can see that now."

"I don't feel that I can take you into the meadow to meet her, but I don't want to miss a minute with her if I don't have to; so if you will excuse me . . ."

"No problem, big brother, I certainly understand. I gotta get going anyway. I'm late making this last delivery."

Dan strode off toward the meadow with long hurrying strides. David watched the two of them as Amy rose from her spot under the tree to meet Dan. The two of them embraced. They looked more as one than two, and somehow David was sure they really were just one. How wonderful for his brother. Instead of feeling strange about the whole thing, he was delighted that he had gotten to glimpse the lady and even more thrilled for his brother to be with her.

Dan put the nickel in the frame with the sketch that night. He realized that these would be the only two material things he was every likely to have of Amy. But her love and this nickel and picture were all Dan really needed. The rest, he had stored in his heart.

CHAPTER 14

Town Talk

Often in this world, perfect lovers miss each other either by a block, a city, a state, or even a time.

Amy knew that somehow she and Dan definitely must have belonged together. Their hearts were so intertwined that she could feel his presence all day as she went about her daily life in 2006. She got up in the mornings, had coffee, went to the shop, or spent her day painting but always with the feeling that Dan was by her side. Somehow even though they managed to only spend a short time each day actually touching, she could feel him in her mind at any time she chose. Realizing that being with him physically on any permanent basis was surely impossible, Amy remained content to take whatever she could get and hold him in her heart all the other times.

Dan felt the same. Somehow the timing had been wrong. It had placed two lovers mistakenly in the wrong centuries yet had managed to reunite them there in the meadow. Leigh Hunt wrote, "There are two worlds; the world that we can measure with line and rule, and the world that we feel with our hearts and imagination." That was how Dan saw it. One world was his farm and his work, but the other world was Amy and the meadow. That was the world—his heart and imagination—that made the other world bearable.

He went through his day—content and happy—feeling Amy with him all the time. The greatest thing was his knowledge that at the end or sometimes even in the middle of his day, he would be able to spend some short time with her. If that was all they could manage to have, then he was satisfied with that. Just the knowledge that such a love was possible meant the world to him and gave him great satisfaction.

Evenings would come. Amy and Dan would meet. The amazing tenderness with which Dan held her gave her enough strength to get through every day without him, and the love he felt flowing from her in return did the same for him. Some nights they said little. They would walk through the meadow hand in hand, sit by the brook, and listen to the gurgling water as it flowed along. Amy watched the sunlight dance on the water; for Dan, it was moonlight dancing on that same water. They felt passion that neither had ever thought possible. It was a passion that went deeper that any sexual encounter. It was a soul-binding passion that transverses time and space. How this had all happened, neither could possibly understand; but what they both felt was easy for them to accept, and both were grateful for the chance in a lifetime to experience such emotion and connection.

They would talk, laugh, and share secrets in quiet happy voices until Amy drifted away; but neither dared to think about or question how much longer they would continue to meet this way. It was something neither wanted to face. Summer was drawing to a close, and Dan had some serious concerns about how he would be able to sit in the meadow all winter. He didn't know how much longer his defective heart would hold out. Amy had no way of knowing with each new meditation session whether she would get to the meadow or not. She had no way of knowing if she would continue to find Dan there on her arrival. They were the few topics they never wanted to discuss with each other.

Jake had mentioned something about a woman in the meadow in town, and that was all it had taken to get people to talking. The ones who would stop by for a visit often looked out into the field, checking to see if there was anyone there. The lean-to Dan had built for protection from the elements did little to stop the wagging tongues. Stories began to swirl around town. Like all small towns, the story grew as it went around. No one dared ask Dan what he thought was going on. It was more fun for the townsfolk to create their own version, and that they did. Some of the stories became totally outrageous.

"Amy, you have gained quite the following around town, you know." Dan laughed one evening as they sat together.

He had a wonderful laugh, Amy thought. She was sure it wasn't heard often. "How so?"

"Jake mentioned some lady in my field, and everyone in town has created their own story about you. They are all afraid to ask me about you, so they just continue to make up more and more stories. David reports all the new ones every time he comes by. You have become a real celebrity around these parts."

"I am so sorry." She hated to have Dan made the laughing stock of the town or have anyone think he was anything but an honest, hardworking, logical man.

"I don't mind at all. Three months ago, if this had happened, I would have been terribly upset. Now I find it all mildly amusing. They are still my friends. They are just having great fun creating stories. They could ask me about it, but they chose to just make up stories for themselves. That is more fun, I think."

"I could stop coming. That might stop them."

"No one can see you even when you are here. I have already tested that one out. I couldn't bear it if you stopped coming. Please don't. I don't know if I could bear life if you weren't in it."

"I was just trying to save your reputation."

Dan laughed out loud at that thought. "I never thought of myself as having a reputation to save. Certainly, the thought that some lady might be my salvation never occurred to me either."

Dan was being honest with Amy. He really didn't mind his friends speculating about who might or might not be in his meadow. It gave him more company as of late. More and more people would stop by to see if there was really something going on. Of course, no one ever saw a lady; but they did see the half tree house Dan had built around the tree.

"What is that stuff you built around your tree?" they would always ask.

Dan thought it best to make some sense of it all for them, so he had created a logical story for them. "I often like to sit there and visit Sue May and our son. Even if I can't see them, the meadow is so peaceful I can almost feel them. Those structures keep me dry and warm while I'm visiting."

It made sense, but no one really believed him. A logical explanation wasn't what they were looking for. They really wanted to hear about a ghost lady. Dan wasn't about to oblige them. After each visitor, he would shake his head and laugh to himself. He didn't remember ever thinking life was this much fun before, but now, he was having a great time. He always tried to imagine what they were thinking was going on in his meadow when they went away. If there was one thing Amy had done for him, it was help him see the funny side to life. That was something he had never done before.

He didn't mind the neighbors laughing or even thinking he had lost his senses, but he was worried about the small sketch, which hung on his wall.

"David," he said one afternoon, "when something happens to me, please take away the picture of Amy in the meadow before the neighbors have a chance to come in here and see it. I would be sad if that were found, and they scorned the whole idea."

"Nothings going to happen to you, big brother, but I will certainly remove the picture right away if anything should. I have never even told

Becky about all this. If I had to take that picture home, it would call for some tall explaining."

Dan laughed at the thought of David trying to explain it all to Becky. "What I would like to hear would be the explanation of why you never told it all to her before."

"That won't be easy. I don't think I have ever really kept much from Becky."

"Why are we discussing this anyway? You are going to outlive me."

"Maybe, but that picture is the only thing I have that holds any value for me; and I wanted to be sure it was not misplaced."

"There is also a small book in the drawer there by the bed. You might be interested in reading it sometime yourself."

"OK, I'll take it out too. David was barely paying attention by now. He found the whole conversation to be a waste of time. Dan was going to live forever especially with Amy here to give him something to truly live for.

Dan wasn't going to tell David about the reoccurring spells either, but he wanted to be sure the picture wasn't out for public display when something happened to him. He wanted to protect the meadow and Amy at all cost.

CHAPTER 15

Dan Departs

It was late August. The weather was sultry, and Amy had been unusually tired lately. She had missed getting to the meadow this night because she had fallen asleep. Suddenly, she awoke, feeling someone was in the room with her. How strange. There was no adrenaline rush, no knot of fear in her throat, and no horror that some stranger had invaded her bedroom. Yet someone was there with her, sitting on the edge of her bed.

"Dan! How did on earth could you get here?" Never in all these months had Dan been able to come to her; only she to him. How had he managed to find her, and what did he want?

"I don't know. I was sitting in the meadow, waiting for you; and suddenly, I felt a rush, and here I was." "I am so glad to see you. I always dreamed of this day when you perhaps could come to me."

"I don't think I can stay."

"Why not?"

"I'm not sure, but something tells me I have only come to tell you how much I love you and that I am going home."

"Home?"

"Yes, Amy, I believe I am really going home. I needed to let you know before I leave how very much you have meant to me, what peace and love you brought to my heart and soul, and how complete you made my life. I would have never known how deeply one could love or how completely one could immerse themselves into another unless you had come to me, Amy."

"Oh, Dan, you know that is exactly how I feel as well." She felt his arms encircle her with their warmth and security. "Please don't leave me."

"I don't believe I have a choice." Dan glanced up at the picture hanging over Amy's bed. "That is an excellent likeness of the meadow. The painting itself speaks quietude and love. You did a beautiful job with it."

"Thank you. It was easy to paint it. It is such a beautiful place."

"Amy, I know how much you love to paint, and I know that sometimes you sell a painting; so I am asking you to paint the meadow. Paint it from different directions. Paint with all the love and peace that is in your heart. Those paintings will sell; of that I am sure. Many will want to gaze on such a peaceful spot and feel that same calmness and love we have felt. Barns are nice, but people need to know there is such a quiet and serene place as that which we hold dear."

"It has always been such a personal place for me. I never thought of putting it on display."

"I believe it is the thing to do. By painting the meadow, Amy, you will keep us together forever. Our memory will live for years to come."

He leaned forward and softly kissed her with the gentleness and love she had always felt from him. "I feel sure that I won't be able to get back to the meadow, but I am hoping I have left enough of my love for you there that it will remain with you no matter how often you visit. Good-bye, my love."

The alarm was buzzing, and Amy reached to turn it off when she remembered Dan sitting on her bed the night before. There was a heavy feeling in her heart. Amy was sure Dan had been right—that he would not be in the meadow again and that she would never see him again. She sat over her coffee trying to analyze the events of the night before. Sadness engulfed her in the morning hour as she had never felt before. The only logical answer was that Dan had somehow died during the night, and his spirit had found hers to say good-bye.

She called Nikki.

"Hi, Mom. You sound dreadful."

"I think Dan has died, Nikki."

"You think what?"

"I believe he is dead."

"What on earth would make you say a thing like that?"

Amy told Nikki of the visit she had had from Dan. Her daughter was saddened because she felt sure her mother was right. She was very worried now. How would her mother take two losses in the same year?

"Are you going to be OK, Mom?"

"Yes, Nikki, I will be just fine."

"When your father died, I felt alone, abandoned, but not terribly sorrowful. I had lost a companion and a friend but not a lover. Joe left me emotionally years ago and married his career."

"Mother, what a dreadful thing to say."

"No, it was fine. We had a good relationship even with the hard times."
"What about losing Dan?"
"I am very sad, but somehow I don't feel like I have lost him."
"What do you mean?"
"I mean, I feel his presence still. It's almost like he is still here somehow, still looking for me. I believe that someday we may find each other again, but I don't know what makes me feel that—just something deep inside my heart."

As the days passed, reality mixed with imagination. Amy began to wonder if the meadow was a real place or if it was still just a place she had imagined and created for herself. She felt that Dan almost had to be a creation on her own. No man could have been so perfect, so caring, and so loving. No love could have been so binding. It must have all been a dream. She must have created Dan when she needed someone and let him go when she had gained strength she needed to keep going. She felt a great lonesomeness that was mixed with a feeling of anticipation. Maybe someday she would find him again.

She began to paint the meadow. Dan had been right. The more she painted the meadow, the more of Dan's love she seemed to feel surrounding her. Maybe this wasn't a dream after all.

For the next year, Amy had painted nothing but the meadow. She had painted it from every angle. She had painted every detail that she could remember. She had poured into her paintings all the peace and love that she had felt there with Dan, and he had been right. The paintings of the beautiful meadow were selling as fast as she could complete them. Maybe it was that need in every one to have a private place all their own to go and rest and escape, or maybe it was just the love that seemed to pour from the meadow. Either way, the pictures did seem to have an effect on almost every one who viewed them. She had painted them with no one there, and she had painted them with her coming across in her white dress; and she had painted them with the two of them sitting under the tree—peaceful and still.

Sadly, the paintings were all she had left of the meadow; for try as she might, no amount of meditation would take her back to that lovely meadow. She never knew if it was because Dan was no longer there or because she just couldn't go there without him. Maybe the concentration just wasn't there anymore. What

ever the reason the meadow seemed lost to her forever except in her paintings. That, for her, was sad; but painting the meadow gave her solace and peace. It was something she could do for herself and for others. Most of all, it was something she could do for Dan.

Dan had died that night from a heart attack. David had gone by early that morning to help him take the last couple benches for Rhonda Hall to town, and he saw him lying in the meadow.

"It was his heart, you know."

"Yes, we knew he was living on borrowed time."

"Amazing he survived all these years. That heart should have given out when he was a child."

"I'm sure glad it didn't. He was the best brother a guy could have asked for."

"Did he ever mention anything about some woman wandering his farm? Most all the county folks have been a buzzing about it for months now."

"Yeah. He thought it might have been a neighbor, but he never saw her more than once, I don't think. You know how those things can get started and keep on going. I think he even enjoyed all the stories circulating around."

"You could be right. Funny, but I noticed your brother seemed to gain a sense of humor this summer. I never noticed that in him before."

"Guess you never get too old to learn."

"Well, he will be missed. Your brother was a hardworking, honest man, David. I am sorry he is gone."

"Thanks, Doc, I am too."

David located the picture hanging on the bedroom wall. The 2006 nickel was in the front of the picture. Dan felt the wise thing to do would be to put the nickel behind the picture so no one would ever see it. They might all ask who the lady was and where the drawing came from; but if the nickel was there, now that would bring up some serious questions that David wasn't ready to answer. Even if he had been willing to answer the questions, he didn't have any answers; so he slid the picture out of its frame and dropped the nickel into a safe resting place behind the paper. In the top drawer of the nightstand, he also found a strange-looking little book. The words on the front read, United Souls Through the Ages. It felt strange holding the small book, and he was sure it had something to do with Dan and Amy's ability to find each other; so he removed it from the home as well. He carried the little picture home and hung it on the wall in the bedroom at home. He slid the book into a small box on his study shelf. Later, he would read it for any hints of what had happened, and then he would tell Becky the whole story.

He was grateful to that lady for giving his brother the joy he had felt—the wonderful love they had shared. She had even given him a sense of humor. How sad they had missed each other, but how wonderful to have been able to unite in such a beautiful place. He would miss Dan very much.

CHAPTER 16

Young John

John had heard stories about his great-uncle Dan ever since he could remember. He had also heard rumors about some lady who wandered the meadow on Uncle Dan's farm and the mystery surrounding her. Some folks said she was the ghost of his dead wife; some thought she was a backwoods lady who no one ever really got to know. There were many theories and suppositions involving his great uncle and the lady of mysterious appearing. Despite his grandfather's efforts to quell such stories, they somehow had gotten out.

His grandpa once told him the story about the lady; the true story, he said.
"Was there really a lady, Grandpa?"
"Oh, yes, there certainly was."
"Did she have a name?"
"Of course, she did. It was Amy."
"Where did she come from?"
"Somewhere in Charlotte, I believe."
"Then why didn't she and Uncle Dan just get married?"
"Well, son, she lived in a different time in history; and it wasn't possible for them to live together."
"What do you mean?"
Then Grandpa would launch into the long story about how love could span space and time and how he had proof of that. He would tell how a woman from the year 2006 had come back in time to walk through Uncle Dan's meadow and sit with him and love him. No one ever knew what proof he was always talking about, and he never told anyone what it might be. Everyone just thought he was defending his brother's reputation. No one really believed he had actual proof. He hung that picture on his bedroom wall that Uncle Dan had held so dear.

The picture of the meadow was just a sketch really of the meadow with a lady walking in it, but it had a special appeal. It didn't really seem to be any kind of proof because anyone could have drawn it, but Grandpa always insisted the woman who came to meet Uncle Dan had drawn it for him.

"Why, look at the date he would say. That should convince anyone."

There were initials AMB and a date '06. That could have been 1906, but even that did seem a bit odd since Uncle Dan has passed away in 1905. Still, it certainly wasn't what any of us considered proof.

Sometimes Grandpa would go into great detail to explain to John how the lady could get there from 2006.

"Meditation was the key to the whole thing."

"You mean, she would just think herself into the meadow?" John would ask with wide-eyed amazement. He wished he could just think himself into all kinds of places. Sometimes he imagined he was a cowboy fighting the Indians or a pirate out on the open sea, but he never actually went anywhere. Those fantasies were just in his mind.

"Maybe it wasn't quite that simple, son; but yes, that is just about how she got there as I understand it."

"Like an imagination?"

"Yes, I guess it was a lot like imagination."

"Did you ever see her?

"Only once. I saw her plain as day, walking right across the meadow into Dan's arms. I remember how happy I was for him to have found such love."

John often would gaze at the picture there over Grandpa's bed and visualize himself meeting the lady and discovering the true story surrounding the mystery.

"When I get to 2006, Grandpa, I will find that lady and prove your story."

"By then, John, you should be just about her age."

"Do you think she will still be there?"

"I bet she will if you just look."

He made himself a pinky promise to find that lady and marry her. He had done the math, and if he and Grandpa were right, she would be his age when he found her. Time went by, and John grew up, left home for the city, and left the lady and the meadow far behind.

By the time his grandpa died, John had graduated from college and started his life in downtown Charlotte. He missed the farm but preferred the big city life, and Charlotte was growing fast. He had purchased an old office building downtown and developed an apartment on the top floor for living and working. He returned to the old home to help his mother organize and dispose of the contents in the home. The only male heir, Grandpa had left the family farm to John. Included in that package was the old home site of great uncle Dan and the infamous meadow. It was hard cleaning out his grandfather's home. John had spent a good bit of his young life under Grandpa David's elbow. Now he was gone. The one thing that caught his eye was that picture still hanging there. It just seemed to be calling to him to join the woman in the meadow.

"Could I have this picture, Mom? I doubt that anyone else would want it."

"Sure,"—she laughed—"you should carry on the crazy uncle tradition. You look very much like him."

"Do you really think he was crazy?"

His mother stopped packing the box she was working on and looked up at him. "No, John. I think he truly found love in the meadow wherever she came from."

"I wish I could find a love that strong."

"I would wish that for every one. Most people look a lifetime for meaningful love, but few find it."

"I think I will wait for that lady in the picture. If I look a lot like Uncle Dan, maybe she could love me the same way."

His mother laughed at that thought. "Don't spend too much time looking for her. I doubt that she is still out there anywhere."

John knew his mother was probably right, but somehow that didn't matter. Deep in his heart, he knew that he had to wait for Amy no matter how long it took."

Back at home, John found just the right spot over his desk that suited the sketch and hung it up. Every day he would look at that picture. He would often turn his chair around, prop up his feet on the desk, and try to imagine that lady appearing and disappearing from the meadow. He tried to imagine how his Uncle Dan had felt seeing her sitting there in the meadow. Most of all, he tried to feel the love he had heard his grandfather describe—a love that was strong enough to reach through time and space and unite two people who were meant to be together; that definitely was the only kind of love John wanted. He wanted to feel a love that was that strong and that binding. As the days passed, he felt himself drawn more and more into the picture. He felt as though he were bonding with the woman who was but a tiny sketch in a big meadow. It was beyond explanation, but it was very real to John.

It was late one evening. John was tired. He had been working on those plans for hours, and now he stopped work and studied the little picture above his desk. He often did this, but tonight the light that hit the little picture caused it to appear damaged. He had never noticed that before. There was a bump, or maybe it was a scrape on the picture that he had never noticed before.

Taking the picture from the wall, he examined it more closely. It showed no damage, but something appeared to be lodged behind the picture. John carefully removed the print from its frame so as not to damage it. Behind the picture was a coin. Not one he had ever seen before but a US coin. He checked the date: 2006. It was a nickel—a very unusual-looking nickel, and it was dated 2006.

It was a strange sensation that John felt come over him. How did Grandpa get a coin dated 2006 when this was only 1982 now, and how long had it been behind that picture? Did his grandpa even know it was there? Of course, he knew. That was the proof he had always said he had. Maybe Uncle Dan had put it there, but Grandpa knew it was there and never showed it to a soul, not even him. That meant the date on the picture really was what Grandpa had said.

He sat on the floor, contemplating this for a long time. Slowly, in his mind, he began to put the pieces together. The lady walking though Uncle Dan's meadow actually was real, and she did come from the future. His grandpa just kept his silence about it all because it was better that way. How would it have helped if Grandpa had produced the proof? No one really needed to know for sure. He guessed his grandpa and Uncle Dan must have enjoyed hearing all the wild stories people had made up over the years. Now John realized that somewhere out there in the year 2006, this lovely lady was living a life and going though daily routines. How old was she? Where would she be when he got there? Was she still walking though the meadow?

Years went by. John became incredibly busy. He never really looked for love. An eligible bachelor was hard to find. Someone was always trying to arrange something for him, but his pat answer was always, "I have already promised my heart to someone in 2006."

Josh Andrews had been his best friend in college. Grandpa's farm was bigger than anyone in the family wanted, so John had developed it into plots and invited Josh to go into the building business with him. They made a great team and were quite successful.

Josh had a pretty wife, Susie, who was always trying to get John involved with one of her single friends.

"Thanks, Susie, but I gave my heart away a long time ago."

"Maybe you could get it back and give it to one of my friends," Susie would tease him.

Josh had often noticed the sketch behind John's desk with a tiny lady in a meadow. One night, he had pulled John aside after the joking and looked very serious. "Have you been kidding all these years about that woman in the meadow, or are you really serious?"

The worried tone he used concerned John, and he didn't want Josh to think he wasn't OK, so he replied carelessly, "It's a standing joke from my family, Josh. No reason for you to be worried about me. If I wanted a date, I would find one myself."

"OK, buddy, but you do worry me sometimes with that talk."

No one really understood the joke, but they always laughed it off and assumed that he just didn't want to be matched up. He never told anyone how serious he really was. He never quite understood why or how, but he felt somehow bonded to that lady in the meadow. He sometimes did what his uncle had done so many years ago. He would go and just sit in the meadow, watching the brook and hoping that the lady would just by chance show up. But she never came, and his life moved on.

John had worked hard to get where he was. His parents, grandparents and great-grandparents had farmed the land. They had owned quite an extensive farm in North Carolina, but farming had never really been in his blood. He had always leaned toward the big city and something to do with building. After college he had headed for Charlotte to build. Now he was doing just that. He and Josh had built a large successful business and made some very wise choices. They built quality homes and had chosen well the areas to build in and types of homes to build. If success was to be measured in money and reputation, then John was at the top of the city's list.

Climbing that success ladder had left little time for a family. He had told everyone including himself that not everyone was meant to live with someone or have a family. Somehow, though, lately he was not entirely at peace with that choice. At sixty-two, he was on the downhill side of life, he thought, and concerned at the prospect of going home alone every night. Maybe he should get a dog. That lady in white from the meadow had never materialized, and he was about to grow old alone.

Dan had sold off almost of the farm now. He had divided it up into subdivision plots and built home after home after home on it. It was an excellent area for home building—not too far from the city yet not too close. He had kept his dad's home and a few acres around it, and he had kept Uncle Dan's home and the meadow partly because Uncle Dan and his family were buried there; but mostly because he never gave up hope that someday he too would get a chance to see the woman in white walking though the meadow.

John and his partner Josh Andrews were still pouring over the last of the newest subdivision plans when the clock struck 9:00 p.m. "Wow," Josh said,

"I didn't realize it had gotten so late. Susie will be worried sick. I better give her a call and let her know I'm on my way home."

Straightening up, his eye caught the picture behind John's desk. All these years, it had hung there, and Josh had never really paid much attention to it. Now he whistled.

"What is it?" John asked.

"Well, that is more than just a little interesting. There is a picture almost exactly like that; only it's a painting in the gallery down on Second and Grand."

"Where is it on Second and Grand?"

"You know, that little gallery by the coffee shop? I swear it looks to be the identical picture."

Josh was still standing there, staring at the little sketch, but John wasted no time. He was out of the office and headed down the street. He had to see for himself.

The gallery was something he passed every day on his way to the office. He had always just glanced at the displays and hurried on his way, but tonight, something in the window stopped him cold. Josh was right! There it was just as he had said it was. There on a stand in the front window was an amazing picture of a meadow with a babbling brook and a tall willow oak tree. The peace and serenity seemed to engulf the viewer, drawing them into the picture and giving them a strange sense of strength and calm. There was a lady in white, coming across the meadow on her way to the tree with white hat in hand and hair gently blowing. The little light over the painting that illuminated it gave an added look of quietude to the picture. John just stood there looking at the picture not knowing how he felt. Years of secretly longing for and loving that strange woman and wondering if she would be here in 2006, and here it was 2007, and there she was. Or at least there was someone who must have known her. Someone who surely had seen this meadow for it was exactly as it appeared today. How could he find her? Through the window, he could see a small stack of business cards beside the easel. First thing in the morning, he would stop in there and retrieve one of those and find out who painted this picture.

The night was endless. Sleep never came. His heart raced at the prospect of possibly meeting the same lady that his great-uncle Dan had been so in love with—the lady who had captured his heart when he was a teen and had never really let it go.

He was at the gallery when they opened.

CHAPTER 17

The Painting

John took the time to go into the gallery today. He examined the picture of the meadow more closely. It was signed AMB '07. He felt his heart beating in his ears. That was the same way the sketch was signed that hung behind his desk; the same one that his grandfather had held on to all those years, but this one was a year later.

He made some hurried inquiries about the picture on display: who did the painting and were they local. The gallery attendant was very helpful and gave John some background on the artist and her other works. He gave John a business card from the small rack beside the painting that the artist had left and suggested if he had further questions, he might contact her directly.

Contact her directly. Of course, he was going to do that. In all the years, he had joked about the lady in 2006; he never truly believed she would be there. Now suddenly, not only was she here, but he was going to contact her. He had meetings all morning; but later this afternoon, he would call her. He had some very serious questions about that picture.

She had just gotten in from the shop, and selling yet one more picture of the meadow. It had been an exceptionally long day, and Amy was ready for some rest and solitude. The phone was ringing. She considered not picking it up, but for some reason, it seemed to be ringing with more urgency than usual.

"Hello," she said, trying to hide the weariness in her voice.

"Amy Brashton?"

"Yes? This is she." A strange feeling crept over her. She recognized that voice, but she just couldn't place who it belonged to.

"I got your card from the gallery in town." The voice went on. "That little gallery down on Second and Grand."

"Yes?" She was still waiting for him to say something like, "You know me; I'm whoever." Who was this? Why couldn't she put a name to a voice that was so familiar?

"It's about that picture of the meadow that you painted."

"Which one?"

"What do you mean which one?" He had only seen one picture of the meadow, and it looked exactly like one he already had hanging on his wall.

"I have only painted the meadow this last year; nothing else. I have painted it from several viewpoints. Some have people in them, and some don't. Was there a number on the bottom of the picture?"

"Oh, I don't know. I didn't notice one. I was too busy looking at the picture. Could we meet at the gallery? I would like to take you to lunch and discuss buying several of these pictures."

"Certainly, would Wednesday be OK?" Amy was always ready to sell pictures of the meadow. She loved people to appreciate the lovely spot as much as she did. She was equally glad that he might be interested in more than one picture, but her week was full with only Wednesday open.

"Yes, if that is the earliest you are able to make it, then that will have to do. I will be there Wednesday at 12:00 noon."

"I will meet you at the gallery then at noon on Wednesday. Thank you for your interest. I didn't get your name."

"John. John Kerr. See you then." He was gone.

Amy felt her heart leap into her throat. She was sure if she didn't sit down she was going to pass out. Ten minutes ago, she had been too tired to even talk to anyone; now she was wide-awake with her heart pounding and her head spinning. She hadn't known why she had such a funny feeling when the man had said her name, but now she realized why. He had Dan's voice—that low deep-throated soft voice that could calm a storm and soothe a soul, and he also had Dan's last name. She knew without wondering there was a connection, but what that could possibly be was a total mystery to her. Wednesday might never get here.

Of course, she knew him instantly. He was waiting for her in front of the picture. He looked exactly as she had imagined he would—very much like Dan but a much more modern version. He still had that rugged, outdoor look, but he was much more suave and sophisticated—sure of himself. Dan never had children, so who was he, where did he come from, and how did he look and sound so much like Dan?

John sized up the lady coming toward him. She was just about his age, he guessed; she was pleasant-looking, and she somehow appeared more peaceful than most of the hurrying people John was acquainted with. He was not one to make a lot of small talk, so he got right to the point.

"How did you come to paint that meadow, Ms. Brashton?"

"It's a long story, Mr. Kerr. How long do you have?" she said, laughing lightly and thinking it would take quite a time to make anyone understand about the meadow. His look was serious. He had that same frown of seriousness that Dan always seemed to have even when they were happy.

"I have all night, maybe even tomorrow. Could I hear your story please?"

"Why are you interested?" she asked; her curiosity peaking now.

"I guess that's a fair enough question. That meadow is on some property that has been in my family for some 150 years now. It is way off the beaten path and, to my knowledge, has never been on any ground open to the public. My grandfather's brother lived on the farm and worked it. He, his wife, and son were buried in that meadow.

"Yes,"—looking at the picture with faraway eyes—"I did not know for sure he was there, but I believe his wife and baby are buried here," and she pointed to the spot where they lay. In the picture, she had omitted the marker stones.

The astonishment in his eyes was genuine. He continued on more slowly now. "They said he went crazy after his wife died and used to see a woman in white coming through his meadow. He even built a lean-to around that tree and would sit there for hours. Some folks thought he was seeing his dead wife; others thought maybe it was someone else's ghost. My grandfather always swore there really was a lady who came to visit him. He spent more and more time there until one night; apparently, he went down to the meadow, and maybe from loneliness or maybe from just being tired of being alone, his heart stopped. They buried him next to his wife. He had been living on borrowed time since he was a child. He had some kind of heart problem; I don't know what. I guess the defect finally caught up with him."

Amy could barely whisper. "Please, could we go somewhere and get some coffee. Maybe you and I need to talk."

There was a small coffee shop attached to the museum. No one was there that time of afternoon, so John and Amy chose a table in the back where they could continue their conversation.

John opened the leather case he had been carrying. He pulled a paper from it. Amy felt her heart stand still. There, lying on the table, was the pencil sketch she had done of the meadow for Dan—complete with lady and white hat.

"My grandfather took this home with him from Uncle Dan's house the night he died. It hung on his wall until the night he died, and then I became its owner. Tales of crazy Uncle Dan came along with the picture, but since I was a teenager, I have been in love with this lady. Maybe I was just in love with the idea of a love that could bind two people so completely that they didn't care what the world thought, or maybe I just craved the peace and solitude that seemed to be connected to her and the love my great-uncle felt for her. While my life was hectic and rushing by me with no love at all, I had this picture to remind me that somewhere there was peace and love. Suddenly, I discovered in the gallery window your picture, which was almost the identical picture. Surely, you can imagine my surprise and the reason I had to find out the story behind it.

Amy had no idea how it all happened; but by now, she was fully aware of what really had taken place. There in front of her, with only slight changes, sat the man she had loved so deeply and lost. There was the sketch she had done less than a year and a half ago, and yet it had been passed down now for one hundred years; she noticed she had dated the painting and remembered that that was when she found out exactly how far apart she and Dan really were—101 years. Yet no one had noticed that because the '06 would have been right in Dan's life; no one would have known that it was 2006, and not 1906. Her fantasy had come full circle. s

"Just a minute, John, I have some other sketches here at the museum. Could you wait just a minute? I would like to get them."

"Sure, I'll get us a sandwich while you're gone. You want chicken salad or ham and cheese?

"Chicken salad please." And she rounded the corner, leaving the coffee shop.

He watched her disappear around the corner of the shop. Of course, he could wait a minute. After all, hadn't he waited some fifty years or so now? What were a few more minutes? Now that he found this woman, he certainly wasn't going to let her walk out of his life. He was sure his great-uncle Dan had led him to this moment, and he wasn't going to pass it up.

When she returned, she had a smaller frame than the meadow in her hand. She reached the table. She was still holding it with the back to John.

"Would you like to see a picture I drew of your Uncle Dan? Turning the frame around, John felt his breath taken out of him; for there in Amy's hands was what looked like a mirror with him looking right into it. There were a few differences but not many. Amy had made a sketch of Dan, but it was him almost exactly with a slightly different hairdo and a few minor changes.

"I tried to do this from memory, and I was never completely happy with it. Strange, it looks more like you than your great-uncle Dan."

His mother had always said he looked like his great-uncle Dan, but she never said how much he looked like him. This had to be the same woman who had known and loved Dan—one and the same woman who walked in that meadow and was the talk of the town and was now standing directly in front of him in the flesh.

"Wow, Uncle Dan really wasn't crazy after all, was he?" After that, he could think of nothing else to say

Just silence. Amy sat there a few minutes, trying to put all the pieces together.

"No, you're Uncle Dan was far from crazy. He was the kindest, most honest, logical man I ever knew. Where is this meadow, John, if you don't mind my asking?"

John thought she might have been joking since she had been there so many times, but when he looked up, he realized she truly didn't know. He had not realized that she had only been there in her mind and would not know where it was actually located physically.

"Would you like to see it? It isn't far from here."

"Oh, my goodness, yes!"

They drove north from Charlotte, not very far to the old homestead. John had been right. Amy was very surprised by how close to her the meadow actually was. It had been right there all along. What a thrill for her to walk in the same meadow she had always dreamed of—the place she and Dan had spent such wonderful moments. This was the place that had been lost to her since Dan left. Now here she was again as though she had never left it.

She and John walked across the meadow. She had stopped at the edge of the meadow to take off her shoes. She just had to be barefoot once more in the meadow. John smiled to see that. He remembered the picture had a barefoot lady. Shoes in hand, she strolled slowly across the meadow just as she had often done alone. There was still a big oak tree in the meadow though John had said that the house and much of the farm had been lost to highways.

"Could we sit here awhile, or do you need to get back to work soon?"

"No, we can sit here as long as you want. I have been waiting for this opportunity most of my life." He was quite anxious not to let this lady get away anytime soon. He sat down, leaning against the tree, and she lowered herself to a spot quite close to him but not quite touching.

"Where did you come from, Amy? And how did you get here? John was asking the exact question Dan had asked what seemed like so very long ago. Amy felt a wonderful wave of peace and love coming over her that she had always felt here in this very special spot, and this was—she was sure—going to be a very special man.

"This is where I come to find peace, John, and freedom from pain."

BEYOND THE MEADOW

The Meadow—sequel title—Beyond the Meadow

Love is the river of life in this world. Think not that ye know it who stand at the little tinkling rill—the first small fountain. Not until you have gone through the rocky gorges, and not lost the stream; not until you have gone through the meadow, and the stream has widened and deepened until fleets could ride on its bosom; not until beyond the meadow you have come to the unfathomable ocean, and poured your treasures into its depths—not until then can you know what love is.

—Henry Ward Beecher

CHAPTER 1

Nothing in life just happens accidentally. There is always a reason behind every path we take and every road we travel. Even though we stumble blindly along life's road, we are never without guidance or goals. It is often in the afterglow that we realize our goals were met because of an unpredicted turn we made or an unexpected path we traveled. That had always been Elizabeth's theory throughout her life. When her life was a jumble, she was always sure there had to be a reason; and some day she would realize it. When life was going good, she felt the same.

She had recently become a successful writer. Something had prompted her to write a book about two people, separated by time but who managed to find each other in a lovely meadow. It was a pleasant book to read with a happy ending. Apparently, many others had thought so as well, for she was now on the best seller list and had been invited to do book signings in many different places. She was on her way home from one of those now.

She boarded the plane as soon as she could. Normally, she didn't fly first class, but her ticket had somehow gotten upgraded; and she was quite pleased with that. She was going to publish a Barn Calendar for next year with a different one of her barn drawings for each month. She was in the process of trying to finish up the last of them now. Five hours on the plane, should see the completion of the last one; and first class would give her the room to spread out and work. The last one was her favorite. She had found it just off the interstate north of Charlotte.

She let her seat slightly backward and rested her head on her pillow. She wanted to relax just a few minutes before she started the drawing. Her mind wandered to the book she had written and how she came to write it. If you had asked her five years ago or even a year ago about writing a book, she would have laughed. At no time in her life did she ever have aspirations of being a writer. She never liked to write and had never even written a short story. Truth be known, Elizabeth was never much of a reader either. She always seemed to have other things she preferred to do.

One day, a story had come to her from who knew where, and she felt the urge to write it down. It was an interesting enough plot involving two people from different centuries. She had woven in parts of her life with parts of the story. The meadow was actually hers. It was exactly as the story had told and created in her mind as a meditation exercise. The muscle disorder was hers as well. She had moved to Charlotte to be closer to her daughter, and she did love to draw. The rest of the story just came to her in pieces and parts. She remembered the nights she would wake up with conversation in her head that belonged in the story or people or ideas that seemed to all go together. She remembered drawing the face of Dan, the main character, with no idea how he would look and no ability to draw faces. The whole story thing had taken over her life, and somehow she seemed driven to finish the novel. Driven was the word her daughter had used, but she felt more like it had been an obsession. She didn't seem to really have any control over the story at all. She simply wrote down what she would wake up knowing. A few of the facts were hers, but the rest was more like some type of inspiration.

What had started out to be maybe a year long project gave her no rest until she had finished, and it took only three months. She was very glad to have it done. Now, she was sleeping nights again, and life seemed to be back on track. Her daughters had liked her book and urged her to publish it. The next thing she knew it was on the market and selling well.

She had published under a pen name with no picture on her book. Publicity was not something she was anxious to have. She had no intentions of making writing a new career at this stage in her life. She was just glad to have gotten this book out of her system. The pen name was an excellent idea as well. Her publisher had forwarded her all the mail she received. It was amazing how many Dan Kerrs had written her, claiming they were "the one" or a relative of the one in her book. Many others had claimed the meadow and offered to let her come and take pictures; some even wrote, claiming to be Amy. She had never responded to any of them, and eventually, she grew tired of even reading them.

For now, it was five hours of peace and quiet. Hopefully, the trip home would be uneventful; and she could get some work done. She would just rest her eyes a few more minutes then finish the barn.

Waiting in airports was just about Dan's least favorite thing to do, but he had spent many hours doing exactly that. He was a successful real estate promoter and builder. His base office was in Detroit, but twenty years ago, he had purchased a large track of farmland just north of Charlotte, North Carolina. He had opened another office there, and now he spent a great deal of his time flying back and forth between the two. He had an hour to kill today, so he wandered off to find something to eat.

Airport food never held much appeal for him either, so he just ordered coffee and sat thinking. For some reason today, his mind kept wandering back to that land he had purchased and what he had found there. It seemed like a lifetime ago now, but still the images from that summer remained fixed in his heart as though it had just happened.

Just about smack dab in the middle of that track of land had been a meadow. It was unusually green and well kept with a brook that flowed along beside it. He remembered the first time he had found that spot. He had bought the farm, sight unseen, but it had great potential and was in an excellent location. He had flown down to look over the property for himself and, in doing so, had stumbled on this beautiful place. He had felt an immediate sense of peace come over him there. What a welcome change that had been from his usually hustle and bustle life.

He sat down there in the field, leaning against a tree and watching the brook go by when he saw a woman walking across the meadow alone. She was wearing what looked like a nightgown of sorts, carrying a wide-brimmed hat and had no shoes. He was not aware of anyone living anywhere close to the property, and it was a very large piece of land he had bought. She saw him; their eyes locked. He looked around to see where she had come from, but when he looked back, she was gone.

He had not planned to stay in Charlotte at that time, but before the summer was over, he had not only stayed there but established an office and fallen deeply in love with it; and the property had proven to be more profitable than he ever imagined. His life had been turned upside down that summer, and his world had never been the same since.

Sitting in the airport restaurant, he could still remember the tingling undertow of emotion he felt that summer when he first saw Emily. It was the same tingle he had felt when he stopped by the little shop in the airport to buy a book to read on the airplane six months ago. He noticed a small novel there in the stands that took his breath away. There in the new-release rack was a small book. *The Meadow* was the title, and the picture on the front of the book was none other than his meadow. It was beyond explanation, but there it was. The author had apparently written under a pen name, and try as he might for the last three months, he had been unable to locate her.

He desperately wanted to find this woman. He had contacted the publishing company numerous times but with no success. He had located a book signing she was supposed to have in Detroit one weekend, but weather had cancelled her appearance. He carried that book in his brief case. Somehow he was going to locate the author.

Dan had never confided what happened to him to anyone. It was personal and private. He was unable to tell anyone. That summer had held one surprise after another for him, and he had no relative or friend to whom he would have confided those events. It had been twenty years ago now, and still he did not understand how it could have happened. Having read the book, the question now was, how could this woman have gotten so many details of that summer, written them down, and never talked to him? Yes, he must find her. She had to know the answers to all his questions.

He was the last to board the plane. He liked it that way. It was going to be a long flight, and he had plenty of work to get done. He disliked travel, but at least by plane, they did the driving; and he got to work. He always traveled first class. He was a big man and hated to be cramped into a small seat with his laptop and papers. This trip, the plane was full to capacity. The only seat left now was his.

Usually, he didn't feel light-headed, but suddenly he felt his knees weaken; and the blood rush to his head. He had never fainted before, but he was sure this was how it felt just before one went down. The attendants realized at once he was in trouble.

"Are you all right, sir? You are very pale." She supported his arm and motioned to the other attendant to do the same on his other side. They helped him to his seat and brought him something to drink. Dan was regaining his composure.

"Yes, thank you, I think I am OK now. I don't know what happened there. Must have been something I ate." *Liar!* he thought. He knew exactly what happened. There, right there on the plane was a lady sitting in the seat next to his who made his knees buckle and his head reel. She looked almost like an older version of someone he had loved and lost. He was sure if she had lived, she would have looked just like this woman. She had the same stubborn jawline and the same dark hair. She seemed to be sleeping, unaware of his predicament. The plane lifted off, and he sat there, studying her intently. This had to be the woman who had penned the book—the woman he had been searching for. She was drawing barns. She looked like Emily; it had to be her.

Her eyes fluttered open. She jumped slightly.

"Oh my." She laughed. "I must have dozed off. Was my mouth hanging open, and drool was running out?"

"No, why would you ask that?" He was embarrassed. He realized he had been staring at her.

"I guess it was the look on your face." She didn't want to stare at him, but he looked very much like the picture of the character she had drawn in her book. She wasn't about to say that since no one knew she was the one who had written the book. She dismissed it as coincidence, but still it was a bit unusual for someone to resemble her character that closely since she had created him completely from her mind. She got out her barn to finish. She realized he was watching her closely.

"Do you like barns?" She was trying to make light conversation. Somehow she was feeling uneasy.

"Yes, I especially like the one you are drawing."

"Thank you. I think it is my favorite. It sits just off I-85, north of Charlotte. For some strange reason, I have always been partial to this particular barn. I am making a calendar for next year of old barns, and this one is going on the front."

"Would you believe me if I told you that was my barn?"

"No." She laughed. "Of course, I don't believe what anyone tells me lately. There is a good reason for that."

"I should introduce myself, but I think I already know who you are."

"Really? Who am I?" Elizabeth was starting to wish she had just kept sleeping. This conversation was really starting to make her uncomfortable now.

"I don't believe I know your real name but your pen name is Ann Thompson, am I correct?"

Bingo. No one had identified her before. Of course, she had been to many book signings now and was becoming more and more visible. That wasn't an advantage. "Yes," she admitted with reluctance, "you caught me. The name is Elizabeth Scott, and your name is?"

"Dan Kerr."

Oh no, Elizabeth thought to herself, *please just make him go away*. There had been several look-alikes at every book signing, and they always wanted some type of publicity. There had been two in particular who had been forcibly removed from the scene by the police. It was more than a little embarrassing. Now here was one sitting next to her on a plane.

"What did you want from me, Mr. Kerr?"

Dan saw where this was going and was quick to avoid it. "Nothing that I can think of. I just happen to have that name. It's not my fault, honestly. My mother did it to me." He tried to laugh and sound casual. Dan wasn't going to say anything at this point to scare her away. He had been looking for this woman for months now, and somehow fate had put them side by side on an airplane going home. What he hadn't expected was for the author of this book to look so much like Emily. He was trying to think of a way to keep connection with her after the plane landed when she interrupted his thoughts.

"Are you going to Charlotte?" Now she was trying to make pleasant small talk. She had not meant to offend him, but she was prepared to ward off any publicity stunt advances.

"Yes, I have a business there and another office in Detroit. I seem to spend more time on planes than I do in the office lately. Is that where you live?"

"I moved there several years ago, and I just love it; but I still don't know my way around." She liked his voice. It was deep and calming with a slight Southern drawl. Interesting, since he was from Detroit that he would sound Southern. "Is this really your barn?"

Now the frown turned to a smile. "Yes, actually it really is." That is a nice view of it, but I believe that the other side looks even better. You have to take the picture from the field and not the road."

"I didn't know how to get there. I didn't see anywhere to turn in when I took this, so I took it from the highway. Often when I take pictures, I am able to pull right up to the barns and walk around them. I didn't see a place to do that with this one."

"Would you like for me to take you there sometime?" Dan was relieved she had believed him. He wasn't after any publicity. That was the last thing he wanted. He did have something he wanted from Elizabeth, but publicity definitely was not it.

"That would be nice really. I could save the front cover for the other side of the barn. Would you have time on this trip to Charlotte?"

What a break. This was his best chance to see her again. Would he have time? If he had no time, he would go out of his way to make time for this lady. He wasn't going to say any more about the barn, but what she didn't realize was that the field from which she needed to take the other view was actually the meadow she had drawn on the front part of her book. He wondered how she would feel when she discovered that. If she thought his looks and name were a publicity stunt, she would avoid him forever if he told her the meadow lay just behind the barn.

"Certainly, I will take the time. How about I call you tomorrow when I can break free, and we will take a ride out there and have some lunch on the way? I have a nine o'clock meeting; that should last a couple hours, then

I'm free all afternoon." Dan handed her a business card. That was to assure her he really was Dan Kerr; and he really was a businessman. Most of all he wanted her to have his phone number. He wrote his cell phone number on the back for good measure.

"That would be very nice, thank you." Elizabeth wrote out her address and phone number for him. The rest of the trip was small talk or no talk. Dan got busy with his work. He wanted to talk and talk to her, but he wasn't sure what he could say now that wouldn't scare her away. It took an enormous amount of self-control to keep all his thoughts and feelings inside. He had so many questions he wanted to ask her. Maybe once she saw the meadow, he could explain it to her; and she would understand. After all, hadn't she been the one to write a book about just exactly what had happened to him? If anyone would understand and explain it all to him, she would.